Taken

ALSO BY KELLI MAINE

No Takebacks

Taken

KELLI MAINE

FOREVER

NEW YORK   BOSTON

Copyright © 2012 by Kelli Maine
Excerpt from *No Takebacks* copyright © 2012 by Kelli Maine
All rights reserved. In accordance with the U.S. Copyright Act of 1976, the scanning, uploading, and electronic sharing of any part of this book without the permission of the publisher is unlawful piracy and theft of the author's intellectual property. If you would like to use material from the book (other than for review purposes), prior written permission must be obtained by contacting the publisher at permissions@hbgusa .com. Thank you for your support of the author's rights.

Forever
Hachette Book Group
237 Park Avenue
New York, NY 10017

www.HachetteBookGroup.com

Printed in the United States of America

RRD-C

Originally published as an ebook.

First Trade Edition: January 2013
10 9 8 7 6 5 4 3 2 1

Forever is an imprint of Grand Central Publishing.
The Forever name and logo are trademarks of Hachette Book Group, Inc.

The Hachette Speakers Bureau provides a wide range of authors for speaking events. To find out more, go to www.hachettespeakersbureau .com or call (866) 376-6591.

The publisher is not responsible for websites (or their content) that are not owned by the publisher.

Library of Congress Control Number: 2012950998

To the king, the queen and the muse. Howard Stern,
E.L. James, and Joe Manganiello.

Acknowledgments

The past five years would've been lonely and miserable if I hadn't wandered into an online writers forum and found the best group of friends an author could ever hope to find. I owe more than I can express to all the past and present members of (here come the acronyms) GGBT, OPWFT, GOTYA, and LB's. Your friendship and support is invaluable.

Taken wouldn't have come together if it weren't for the keen eyes of Krista Ashe, Annie McElfresh, Rebecca Rogers, Melanie Kramer-Santiago, and Chanelle Gray. Rachel A. Marks blew me away with Taken's cover. Her artistic and literary talents are beyond measure.

Thank you to my family for letting me disappear into my pretend worlds and listening while I talk endlessly about people and places that don't exist.

Taken

Prologue

My fingers shake as I log onto the video chat. I can't believe I've made it this far into the interview process with Rocha Enterprises. This is my dream job, and a shot at being the project manager for the renovation of historic Turtle Tear Hotel working for a world-renowned company. It's a bigger opportunity than I ever imagined I'd have.

I've researched Turtle Tear Island and the background of the hotel extensively. There's no way anyone else is a better candidate for the position, and the fact that I made it this far—through the basic human resources interviews to an interview with the CEO himself—is proof of that.

I click my mouse to connect. I'm five minutes early, but my interviewer is already logged into the video chat. My palms become slick with sweat, and I wipe them on my pants.

"Hello, Ms. DeSalvo. I see you're prepared to start early."

Even with my cheap webcam displaying a grainy image, the warm smile greeting me from the screen should put me at ease, but I'm intimidated as all hell. Maybe it's the deep voice that sends prickles of heat down my neck and flushes my cheeks, or the handsome, clean-shaven face. It could be the tidy, slicked back hair that makes this feel so intimidating and all too real.

This can't possibly be real. I have to be dreaming.

The dark, piercing eyes on my monitor are most definitely dreamy.

What am I thinking? This is an interview with the CEO of Rocha Enterprises, not some dating website meet and greet. I have to pull myself together.

"Hello." My voice cracks. I clear my throat, straighten my shoulders and smile. "I'm willing to bet I'm the most prepared applicant you've spoken to."

There. I exude confidence.

My boasting is rewarded with the flicker of an eyebrow and a repressed smirk. "Is that so?"

Oh, that voice sends goose bumps crawling up my arms.

"Maybe you can tell me something I don't know then. Go ahead and impress me, Ms. DeSalvo."

My mind flashes through the dozens of facts I know about the property. Despite my staunch desire to remain professional, my over-eager libido rears its head when my interviewer rubs a long finger over a full bottom lip. Somehow, I find myself reciting the romantic love story of Turtle Tear's founder and his wife instead of something more professionally relevant, like the ecological importance of preserving the integrity of the island.

"Did you know, Mr. Rocha, that Archibald Weston built the hotel to impress a woman?" I wait for a curious lift of the chin in response before I continue. "Mr. Weston was desperate to win the affections of Ingrid Burkhart. He convinced himself that building her a magnificent place to live would win her hand in marriage.

"Turtle Tear Island with its lush green trees and beautiful wild flowers seemed like the perfect place to build it. Archibald grew up in the area and paddled his canoe to the tranquil island every chance he had." I stop to take a breath and to make sure I'm not droning on too long and losing my audience.

That long finger glides across those amazing lips again. Instantly, I imagine how soft and firm they would feel pressed against my own. Why does my webcam image have to be so awful? If I get this job, I'm buying one that displays in high def.

"You're an excellent story-teller, Ms. DeSalvo." A trace of humor mingles with the deep timbre. Could this be a trifecta? Wealthy, good looking *and* a sense of humor? "I'm entranced. Please, continue."

"During the course of Archibald's business ventures, he'd visited the Yucatan and been taken with the Hacienda-style cattle ranches in the region. Turtle Tear Hotel was modeled after a ranch where he'd stayed during one of his visits."

"Is that so?" Those eyes and a strong jawline come closer to the screen.

My story is impressive. I'm nailing this interview.

"Yes, that is so. Anyway, he built Ingrid a grand hotel since the island is remote and he knew she would want friends and family to visit and stay. Once it was completed, he showed up on Ingrid's doorstep, dropped to one knee and instead of proposing, presented her with the deed for Turtle Tear Hotel."

I hear a low, exhaled, "Hmm…" and some shuffling of papers. My screen blurs with movement. "I'm just making notes. Please, go on."

I take a deep breath and squeeze my hands together. The next part is my favorite.

"Archibald told her he'd put his blood, sweat, tears and entire heart into building the home where he wanted to spend the rest of his life, and since she owned his life, it was all hers to have. He only hoped she'd let him keep his soul, which was bound to hers for all eternity."

"Wow. That's an incredible declaration. He was a brave man."

My heart pounds. I'm afraid it can be seen beating against my blouse on the other side of the small camera. "Yes. He was very brave and entirely selfless in his pursuit of Ingrid."

"I assume she accepted since they were married?" The question comes through in a louder, more insistent tone that makes my speakers crackle. Something else to add to my wish list.

"Actually, no. She told him he needed her parents blessing if she was to return to Turtle Tear with him." I clear my throat and can't suppress a grin. "This is where the story gets really interesting."

"It gets *even better*?" My grin is reflected back on a pair of delicious-looking lips framed by deep dimples on both sides. The image pixelates and freezes.

"Much." I fiddle with my webcam cord trying in vain to get a better connection. "Archibald and Ingrid were the Romeo and Juliet of the Civil War. His family supplied sugar cane from their plantation to the Confederate troops. Ingrid's family housed Confederate deserters. Even though it was August, 1865 and the war had ended, there was no way Ingrid's parents were going to give Archibald their blessing to marry their daughter and take her away."

"What did he do?"

Damn. I wish I could see the expression that accompanies the urgency conveyed in the tone of the question, but my screen is still frozen on that set of white teeth and pair of dimples. Not that I mind. I'm considering making it my new screensaver.

"He tried his best for months to convince her parents he was worthy of Ingrid, even offering to let them live at the hotel, too, but they wouldn't budge. Finally, heartbroken with nothing left to lose, he climbed a ladder up to her window one night, broke in and whisked her away.

"Ingrid was furious at first, but when she got to Turtle Tear, it was love at first sight and she refused to ever leave the island again. It's said that she's buried there, but no grave marker has ever been found to confirm that fact."

I sit back in my chair—mirroring your interviewer was a tip I acquired in an interview workshop—and wait for a response.

"That's quite a big risk for the love of a woman. I supposed it paid off for him in the end. Would you agree, Ms. DeSalvo?"

"Yes. The lengths he went to just to win her over...I'm sorry. Ingrid and Archibald's story always overwhelms me." I put a hand to my chest and inhale deeply to catch my breath. "His grand, romantic gesture won him his wife and the home where he lived the rest of his life. I hope to work with your company to restore the property and hotel to its original style and design, to make it a place nobody would ever want to leave."

"Something Archibald and Ingrid would be proud of?"

My chest fills with emotion that can't be repressed. An enormous smile threatens to split my face in half. "I'd love nothing more, Mr. Rocha. Given the opportunity—"

"The opportunity is yours. I've never seen someone so passionate and knowledgeable about a rundown hotel on swamp land in the Everglades. I'd be a fool to entrust anyone less enthusiastic with this project. In fact, you're the only one I'd trust it to. Nobody has proven themselves more deserving."

The rest of the interview becomes a blur. A haze of details and names of H.R. personnel who will be in touch to discuss salary and relocation. My head is in the clouds. My dream realized.

I'm the newest project manager at Rocha Enterprises. The Turtle Tear renovation is mine!

One

Three months later...

The club is packed. Bodies grind together on the dance floor. There's barely room to move. You catch my eye.

You're alone.

Bass pounds through my body, rushes from my head to my toes, takes the same path your eyes follow. Your dark-eyed stare is flutter-soft on my skin. It raises goose bumps. Makes me flush. My vodka and cranberry-soaked blood runs hot with need.

You smile. Dimples pierce your cheeks. Your eyes flash. I can't resist.

"Rach!" Shannon grabs my arm. She's sweaty from dancing and pulls her blonde hair up off her shoulders. "I'm going." She tilts her head toward Shawn or Shane or Seth—I'm not sure—the guy she met two hours ago.

"How am I supposed to get home?" She drove.

Shannon shoves her car keys in my hand. "See you in the morning." She winks and pushes back through the crowd toward the guy whose name starts with an S.

When I turn from watching Shannon go, you're standing right in front of me. "Hi," you say. Familiarity strikes, but I don't think I'd ever forget meeting you.

"Hi." I fall into your dark eyes and can't get out. They're serious and focused on mine. Looking away would be a crime.

You run a hand through your wavy black-brown hair. Are you nervous? I can't tell. "What were you drinking?" You tap my glass, empty except for melting ice.

"Vodka and cranberry." I take in a thick, damp breath. Dancing bodies fog up the air, make it heavy to breathe.

You shake your beer bottle, indicating its emptiness. "I'm headed to the bar. Would you like another?"

I have to drive Shannon's car home, but I don't want to stop talking to you. I nod. "Please." I'll drink slowly. I'll drive even slower.

I follow behind you, taking in the view of your incredible backside in jeans. A black long-sleeved shirt shifts with your strong, wide shoulders and hugs your narrow waist. You work out. *A lot.* The body I'm staring at didn't come from luck and a good gene pool.

You glance back to make sure I'm following. When a group of people push between us, you reach out and take my hand. My fingers curl around yours like they're possessed.

We reach the bar. You squeeze between two men. I stand back to wait while you order. I watch you reach into your pocket. A second later, you turn to me and hand me a glass.

"Thanks." I take a deep drink, ignoring my self-promise to sip and make it last. Looking at you, I need all the courage this vodka is offering.

You sip your beer, watching me. An intense magnetism pulls between us. I'm sweating. I wipe my forehead with the back of my hand. The vodka is kicking in fast. I stumble sideways. You grip my arm.

"Feeling okay?" you ask.

The room spins and tilts. Black spots swim through my vision. "No. I need to sit." My drink slips through my fingers and splatters on my bare leg.

"I've got you." You put an arm around me and lead me toward the door. "You need some air."

I'm blacking out and coming to, over and over again. This has never happened from three and a half vodka and cranberries before. "I need to get home."

"I'll take you," you say.

"No. I…" The words won't come. They buzz around in the darkness inside my mind searching for the light. I watch them break apart and fade.

You usher me through the parking lot. Open the door of a black car. Put me inside. "We'll be home soon," you say, buckling a seatbelt around my waist.

I try to grip the door handle to get out. My arm won't move. My head lulls on my shoulder. The blackness narrows, leaving a small tunnel focused on the dashboard. Then it closes completely.

No more words.

No more light.

No more sound.

Just like that—I'm taken.

Two

My eyelids are heavy, too heavy to lift. Light glows white behind them. I turn toward its source, and it gets even brighter. I crack my eyes open, peel their stickiness apart. Everything's blurry. Light shoots through my head like an electric shock. I cringe and squeeze my eyes shut again.

My mouth is dry. My tongue, stuck to the roof, is limp and swollen. I swallow, but there's no wetness to quench my thirst.

I open my eyes again, slowly this time, just narrow slits to get used to the light. There's a window. All I see is sky, clear and blue. Where am I?

Panic surges through my chest and squeezes tight enough to make me gasp. I don't remember anything—where am I? How did I get here?

I sit up. Ropes tie my hands to the bed. My heart rate speeds, my muscles quake, my eyes dart around the room and land on you.

"You're awake," you say, standing from a leather couch and thumbing a button on a remote to turn off the muted T.V.

I remember you. The club. The *drink*. "You put something in my drink."

Quickly, I take stock of my clothes. Skirt—still on.

Top—still on. Underwear, bra—both in place. My shoes are the only things missing.

"I didn't touch you," you say, coming to the side of the bed and pulling up a straight-back chair. I shift away as far as I can, press my shoulder against the cold windowpane. The bed sits higher than mine at home and it's smaller, narrower. You lean forward and rest your elbows on the mattress.

We stare at one another. Your intense gaze is the same as the last time I saw it—when you drugged me. My chest heaves with the effort of breathing. My heart races. "Why am I tied to the bed?" My voice cracks.

You reach for a bottle of water on the nightstand, twist the cap off and hold it to my lips. "Drink."

I shake my head and pull away. The ropes scratch and burn my wrists.

You smile. "There's nothing in it. I promise."

Your dimples make you look like a nice guy. You're not a nice guy. "I want to go home."

You run your finger underneath the rope and stroke my wrist. "You are home, Rachael."

I try to pull away from you. "Don't touch me!" Sobs roll up my throat and out my mouth. Tears gush from my eyes. "I want to go home!"

You sit back and prop your foot up on your opposite knee, thread your hands behind your head and watch me crumble. Your face is etched with remorse. You close your eyes—I want them open, want you to feel pain and guilt for what you've done to me.

Flames of rage dance in my belly, crackle and roar inside me. I dart for you, thrashing against the ropes. I will kill you. Tear you apart. *"This is fun for you?"* I curl my feet up underneath me and push against the ropes with my toes. *"Let me go! Let me leave!"* I manage to get my teeth on a rope and try to chew my way to freedom.

You reach out and grab my shoulders. "Stop. You're going to hurt yourself."

I lick blood from my torn, raw lips. My wrists bleed. I throw myself back onto the pillow and scream at the top of my lungs. I scream until my eyes throb, until my ears pop, until my voice is only a rasp.

You stand over me and stroke my hair back from my forehead. "Rest," you say, and walk out of the room. I watch you leave hating myself for ever thinking your body was something I wanted.

Why did you take me? Is this human trafficking? Will you sell me as a prostitute, a sex slave? My chest aches, and my breath hitches and shakes. I have to keep it together and find a way out.

I run my eyes over the long, rectangular room. A nightstand sits beside the bed and the chair you sat in. At the end of the bed, a dresser is pushed against the wall. The couch and T.V. make up a sitting area on the opposite side of the room with a matching leather chair and a wood table between them. The ceiling is slanted. I'm held captive in an attic bedroom.

You didn't close the door. I'm not locked in. If I could

get the ropes untied...Does anyone know I'm missing? My phone. Where's my phone? They can track me that way. Did you take it?

My mom will have a break down when they tell her I'm missing. My dad died last year. Her reaction to losing me to a job offer in Florida a few months ago was bad enough to keep me from taking it and leaving Ohio. She won't make it through this.

Shannon's my only hope, but she left before you bought me that drink, before you took me away. Did anyone see us together? Did anyone see us leave? If they flash my picture on T.V., would anyone know where to start looking?

Maybe that's what you were watching for on T.V. Maybe you're paranoid. "I hope they track you down and lock you in a cell for the rest of your miserable life!" I scream. You don't answer.

I close my eyes and try to think. My only way out of here is you. I have to be calm and rational when you return. What do you want with me?

I have no answer. You didn't touch me. I'm clothed. I'm not hurt. Why did you take me? I stare out the window, like it's written somewhere in the bright blue sky.

There's no clock. I don't know how much time has passed before you return. You're carrying a bowl of soup and a pack of crackers. "You need to eat," you say. "Will you let me feed you?"

I don't want food. I want to be untied. "I need to use the bathroom."

You study my face, considering your options.

"You can't come with me," I say, praying you don't.

"If I untie you, will you behave?" You narrow your eyes at me, threatening. "If you don't, I'll have to come in with you."

You set the soup and crackers on the nightstand beside the bottle of water and sit in the chair. "Rachael, can I trust you?"

What makes you think you can trust me? Do you really think I won't run? "Yes."

You hesitate, dark eyes locked on mine. Am I giving anything away?

Slowly, you reach for the rope and untie my wrist closest to you, then reach across and untie the other. Before you can restrain me, I grab the steaming bowl of soup and throw it at you. It hits your chest, and I dart from the bed.

Your reflexes are fast, and mine are slow from being drugged. Your fingers wrap around my arm and yank me back against your wet chest. One strong arm wraps around my shoulders and holds me in place. "That was my fault," you whisper in my ear through clenched teeth. "You're not ready to be untied yet."

You spin me to face you and grip my shoulders. Your dark eyes bore into mine. "Do you need to use the bathroom?"

Hate wells in my chest. I glare back at you then spit in your face. Your fingers squeeze. Your thumbs could crack my collarbone. You close your eyes and breathe out hard. "Get in the bed." You shove me, and I fall back into it.

I grab the ropes before you have a chance, and we grapple with them. You press your forearm into my chest and pin me to the bed. I bite your shoulder. The ropes slide through my fingers and burn like hot liquid as you pull them from me.

I'm tied again. We pant for breath, winded from our struggle.

You collapse back in your chair and shove your fingers through your wavy hair, exasperated. Did you think this would be easy? "Don't look at me like that," you say, and stand to strip off your shirt. Blisters are already puffing out on your smooth chest. My teeth pierced your shoulder. I run my eyes down over your defined abs and turn away as heat pulses through me.

I can't think about you like that. I won't. You're holding me prisoner in your house. What is wrong with me?

I let my eyes roam back to you. This might be my only way out. "Would you untie me to let me touch you?" I whisper.

You study me with a blank expression. "When you touch me, it'll be because you want to, not because you want me to untie you."

A growl, like an animal, rips up my throat. "I will *never* want to touch you. *Never!*"

You ignore me and slip your jeans down over your hips. "I'm going to go wash the soup off. I'll be back, and then we'll try to feed you again."

I watch your bare feet pad out of the bedroom, willing my eyes to stay away from any other parts of your body. Why do you care if I eat? You kidnapped me.

A shower turns on somewhere down the hall. I hear you step in and slide a curtain closed. Something thuds, like a plastic shampoo bottle set down on a ledge. It doesn't take you long to come back with a towel wrapped around your waist, dark curls wet and glistening on your head.

You stand next to the bed, your low-slung towel level with my eyes, and open the drawer to your nightstand. After shuffling around inside, you take out a small white tube and rub some kind of ointment on your chest over the blisters.

"What do you want from me?" I ask. My voice is filled with defeat that's slowly taking over my heart. "I'll do whatever you want." Tears trickle down my cheeks. "Just let me go home."

You bend down and rub your thumbs across my cheeks collecting tears. "I told you, Rachael. You are home." Your warm lips press against my forehead. "It'll be good."

"What do you mean?" I whisper, afraid to ask, because I already know the answer. My lips tug down at the corners and quiver. You're never going to let me leave you.

You sit beside me and run your fingers down my cheek. "You've always been the person holding everything together haven't you?—for your mom when your dad was sick, after he died, for your brainless roommate."

I can't breathe. I can only stare at you. "How do you know about me?"

Your eyes trail over my face. "I know." You stroke my

hair and stare deep into my eyes. "You're always the strong one, aren't you? But who takes care of you, Rachael?"

"I take care of me." I shift my head away from your fingers. "I don't even know you. Were you stalking me?"

You grin, like I'm a little girl asking a silly question. "I offered you a job. You couldn't take it. Your life wasn't your own. Now it can be."

Your voice. Your face. That's it—I know you. "We video chatted. You're…" I shake my head in disbelief. You can't be the clean-shaven man in the business suit I spoke to.

"Merrick Rocha, CEO, Rocha Enterprises." You smooth the crease between my eyebrows and laugh at my shock. "You made a lasting impression on me, Rachael, and I don't like to be turned down. I needed to find out why you didn't come work for me."

How can a respected, beautiful man be entirely crazy? "So you *kidnapped* me?"

You flinch at my words. "I'm *detaining* you until you choose to be here."

My mind races back through everything you've just told me. "But, how does that make my life my own?"

You frown and look away from me. "You want to be here. I know you do." You leave the bed and cross the room to dress. I don't watch. I stare out the window.

Mr. Rocha, real estate mogul and owner of Rocha Enterprises, kidnapped me. My mind tries to make sense of it, but it spins in endless circles. You want me to choose to be here with you. It defies logic.

I think back to my video interview with you. It was the third interview. The two prior had been with a human resources manager. You were impressed with me. I was attracted to you.

You said you didn't even need to consult anyone else for an opinion and offered me the position of project manager right then. You offered to fly me to Florida on the next plane out. I told you I would need to discuss the offer with my family, and called you the next day to decline after my mom freaked at the thought of me leaving town.

It was my dream job overseeing the renovation of a historic hotel in Florida's Everglades with a multi-million dollar budget at my disposal. After years of architecture and design classes, working as an intern for pennies, my day had arrived only to be shot down.

I snap my head to look at you. "We're at Turtle Tear Hotel, aren't we? In the Everglades."

You pull a soft, white t-shirt down over your chest and smile. "I told you, you're home." You step toward the door.

"Wait!" I call after you. You turn and face me. "Why like this?" I tug at my ropes.

You shrug. "I didn't know how else to do it." Your eyes are tormented. "I'm not really a kidnapper, Rachael."

"Then let me go."

Your head drops. "You'll try to leave."

"I don't understand. Why me?"

You don't answer, just shake your head and leave the room.

Three

You untie my right hand to let me eat. I raise the sandwich to my mouth and take a bite. Peanut butter and grape jelly.

"I hope it's okay," you say. "I can make something else if it's not."

I've resolved to act like your best friend in the world until you let me loose, and I can get the hell out of here. "It's actually one of my favorites from when I was a kid. I loved PB&J's all warm and gushy from my lunchbox."

"You want another?" You gesture toward the bag of bread, jar of peanut butter and squeeze bottle of jelly on the nightstand.

"Yes, please. I'm starving."

You laugh and reach for the bread. "You should be. You haven't eaten in over two days."

I gasp and choke. You pat my back and grab the bottle of water. I chug it and cough a few more times. "How long was I out?"

"Since Friday night. It's Monday afternoon."

I drop my sandwich and grip your arm. "You have to let me call my mom. She'll be having a nervous breakdown by now."

You take my hand and hold it between both of yours. "She's fine. I've taken care of it."

"What does that mean? You've taken care of it?" I'm squeezing your hand, holding on for dear life.

You tuck my hair back behind my ear. "Don't worry, Rachael. I've taken care of everything. She's not worried about you."

Thoughts race through my head. I grasp for them, but they slip through my fingers. *"What did you do to my mother?"*

You pick up my sandwich and hand it to me. "Please, Rachael, do you think I'd hurt her? I told you, everything I did, I did for you. I told your mom that your plans to join me here were sudden and you would be in touch soon. Now eat."

"She believed you? That easily?"

He grins, a dimple studs his cheek. "I can be charming and persuasive."

I didn't know my mom could be charmed or persuaded by a man. I take another bite. My throat is constricted, and I'm sure I won't be able to swallow. You pick up the T.V. remote and turn it on. "Any preference?"

I shake my head and wash down my sandwich with a huge amount of water. "Can I see the hotel?" Maybe I'll locate a phone or a vehicle I can steal.

You meet my eyes, considering. "Okay. You seem calm now. It's not like you can go anywhere. The only way off this island is by helicopter. You don't fly, do you?"

"Fly?" My head instantly aches. "No, I don't fly." With my

free hand, I gesture to my bound wrist. "Why am I tied to a bed if I can't get off the island?"

"So you couldn't hurt yourself." One side of your lip quirks into a bashful smile. "Or me."

"Hurt you? You're a lot bigger and stronger than me."

"I was afraid you might go crazy."

I can't do anything but stare at you and blink. "You abduct me and *you* were afraid *I* might go crazy?"

You bite your lips, trying not to laugh. "I never said I was good at this. It's my first time. You have to cut me some slack."

I can't suppress a sharp laugh. It surprises me as much as it does you. "Other than tying my wrists, you suck at this."

You thread your fingers through your hair and rest the palms of your hands on your forehead. "I should have never done it. I'm sorry. It was impulsive and stupid." You let your hands fall and lower to your knees beside me. Your fingers work quickly to untie my bound wrist. When it's free, you hold my hand and look in my eyes. "I didn't know how to get you to come with me."

I can't shake the feeling that you're way ahead of me—that your feelings are more than two people who were attracted to each other in a bar one night. "How long have you been watching me?"

You take a deep breath and look down at my hand in yours. "Since about a week after you turned down the job."

I pull my hand from yours. Your touch isn't welcome. "Three months. That was three months ago."

You nod, but won't look me in the eye. You're ashamed. "I didn't peek in your windows or anything like that. I respected your privacy. Nobody has ever refused a project manager position at Rocha Enterprises. When you told me your situation and turned down my offer to relocate you *and* your mom..." You let out a long breath, and your eyes finally crawl to mine. "My intention was to convince you— in person—to take the job. But after I got to you, after I found out what kind of woman you are, I knew there was nothing I could say and no amount of money I could offer to change your mind. I got desperate."

I stare you down, want to make you flinch under my hard gaze. Your eyes hold steady on mine, up for the challenge. "What kind of woman am I?"

You lift your chin a little more. "Smart, but I knew that from our phone conversation. Beautiful, but a lot of women are." You reach up with a shaky hand and brush my cheek. "Kind and loyal. Caring. Loving. Selfless." You smile watching your fingers trail across my skin. When you meet my cold eyes, your hand falls and your smile falters. "The kind of woman who could have everything she wants if she would only take it for herself. But she won't. That's why I brought you here."

I make a fist, squeeze it tight and pound it against my knee. What were you thinking? "Take me on a tour of this place. I can't think about this anymore."

I was right. You are keeping me in the attic. It's the only part of the hotel that's habitable. Plaster crumbles off the walls. Chipped and broken tile litters the floors. You lead me to the grand staircase. It sweeps in a wide arc from the third floor down to the entryway.

I place my hand on the top of the railing. "That's not secure," you say, putting an arm around my waist to keep me from falling over the side.

"This is mangrove root, isn't it?" I ask, bending to slide my fingers over a twisted wooden baluster.

Your serious, focused gaze is back, appraising me. "Yes. Local to the area. This railing was installed

"During the recovery from the Okeechobee Hurricane in nineteen twenty-eight." I run my hands over the soft, worn wood. "There wasn't much money to rebuild, so they used what they had on-hand."

When I turn back to you, your hands are tucked inside your jeans pockets, and there's a smug smile on your lips.

"What?" I ask.

"My method for getting you here couldn't have been worse, but I knew this place had worked its way inside you like it has me." You run your hand along the railing, stopping beside mine. "Nobody knows its history like you. After our interview, I knew you were the only one I could trust it to."

"What made you buy it?" I take a step down, and you follow beside me. "It's falling apart, there's no access to the island. It'll take a miracle to make this place operational again."

"It doesn't matter. Look at this place." You stop and open your arms wide taking in the soaring ceiling with thick wood beams and colorful peeling Spanish murals of trees, lakes, birds and turtles. "Tell me you don't feel it."

I do feel it. It's magic. Life throbs outside the long, shuttered windows. Tendrils of tender green vines snake through cracks in the foundation, sneak in under doors and climb up window frames. "I feel it," I whisper to myself. But you hear me.

"I knew you did," you whisper back. "Do you know how it got its name? Turtle Tear Island?"

"No. That's the one piece of history I couldn't dig up." I spent hours and hours prepping for my interview with Rocha Enterprises. When I first started researching the historic hotel, I fell instantly for its rustic charm. Turtle Tear was the only place to vacation in the twenties if you were wealthy. Even celebrities stayed on the island for their summers.

I found black and white pictures online of women in cocktail dresses sitting on the tiled patio under the shade of ancient flowering trees. I could almost hear the circular fountain in the center of the patio trickling with water when I stared at the photo. I printed a few pictures and carried them in my day planner until I turned down the job.

"There's a legend," you say starting down the stairs again, "that Ponce de León while searching the Everglades for the Fountain of Youth took a Native American lover and kept her on this island. He promised her when he found the fountain, they would marry, and they'd have children together." You stop to make a point. "I've read theories that Ponce was obsessed with finding the fountain to cure his impotence."

After a shrug, you continue. We're almost to the bottom of the stairs to the grand entryway. "Ponce never found the fountain and never returned to her. This ties in to the name Turtle Tears because when sea turtles lay eggs, they secrete a gel-like substance out of their eyes to clear the sand, but it looks like tears. The tears of turtles laying eggs on the island became connected to the childless lover of Ponce de León alone and abandoned here until her death."

We step off the last stair onto the broken terracotta tiles in the entryway. "If my recollection of middle school history is correct, the story can't be true. Ponce de León was married to a woman named Lenore before he ever came to Florida, and they had kids," I say.

You sigh and step forward, reaching out to pick a flake of red paint off the wall. "Sometimes men make promises they don't intend to keep."

You're lost inside your thoughts. I wander to the other side of the room, dodging debris. A storm must've knocked the window above the door out—shards of glass glitter all over the floor. It sparkles in the sun streaming in from the shattered remains of jagged glass around the frame.

I don't know what to make of you.

I glance back, and you haven't moved. You're still picking paint from the wall, deep in the past somewhere mulling over promises you made and didn't keep? It's then I realize I'm not afraid of you. I don't think I ever was afraid physically. My fear was never getting home.

A wavy lock of hair falls and brushes your cheek. Standing there lost in thought, you look so innocent, so young. "How old are you?" I blurt without thinking.

You turn, startled. I think you forgot I was there with you. "Thirty-two." Only seven years older than me and you've accomplished so much. "Why?" you ask.

You always look so serious, so…alone. I noticed that in photos of you in magazines and online. I wonder if you are alone a lot. "I read about you before my interview, but I didn't know you were so young." For some reason, now I feel like I'm the one who's been spying on you.

You turn and gaze up at the soaring ceiling. "I feel like I'm fifty most days." Your eyes swivel to mine. "God knows I've made enough mistakes to fill fifty years."

You want me to forgive you. You've given me this gift, this dream. You want me to tell you it wasn't a mistake.

I can't. I don't know if I can ever forgive you for drugging me and bringing me here without my knowledge. Tying me up.

Your eyes plead with me. *I did it for you,* they say. But why? I can't understand what would make you take such a chance? You could go to jail if I made one phone call. You could lose everything. "Why did you risk so much? I'm a stranger to you."

You rub your hands together and groan, torn about what to tell me. "I owed it to...let's just say the universe. I owed it to the universe. I had a lot to make up for. I knew how much this place meant to you. I could hear it in your voice over my laptop speakers. I could see it in your eyes and the look on your face. It was more yours than mine. Then I saw you one day..."

You turn toward the window and drag a hand through your hair, tug at the back. "I saw you in a coffee shop near your apartment. You had printouts of photos of this place. When you left, you tore them up and tossed them in the trash. After you got inside your car, I saw you break down in tears and sob against the steering wheel."

You take a few steps toward me. "You needed this place. It needed you. I needed to give it to you. That's it."

I remember that day. Why didn't I see you there? I sat at a table taking my last glimpses of Turtle Tear Hotel, determined to destroy my pictures and smother the hope I'd had of bringing it back to life. Each rip of paper tore through my heart. I couldn't get to my car fast enough so I could melt into a puddle of tears. "You saw me there." It seems surreal to go from that moment to standing here in the grand entryway now.

"I saw you there," you say, shuffling your foot across the shards of glass on the floor.

"Is that when you decided to take me?"

You take a few more tentative steps toward me, glass cracking under your feet. "That's when I knew I had to do something. That's when I got desperate."

My emotions are tangled and warring. For good or bad, you gave me my dream back. Nobody else could see how much taking the job meant to me—nobody cared to see. But you did. A man I spoke to once on the phone. You knew because it meant just as much to you.

I want to hug you, hit you, yell at you, and cry for joy.

You tilt your head and smile softly, like you see all of my pent up emotion written on my face and don't want it to erupt. Slowly, you reach out and run your hand down my arm. "Let's finish the tour. You haven't seen the fountain."

I let you take my hand and lead me down a hallway that runs under the stairs toward the back of the hotel. We enter a lounge. A stone fireplace is built into the corner and two enormous wooden doors sit on the back wall. You take the iron handle on one of the doors and brace your feet apart. When you pull, the muscles in your arms and back tighten and ripple. The muscles in your thighs press against your jeans. The magnetism I felt at the club rushes back. I fight against my desire to touch you—to have you touch me.

The door wrenches open on rusty hinges, letting sun and a blast of hot, humid air inside. You stand back and brush your hands together, getting off the dust and grime. "What do you think?"

I step out into a tropical Eden in the middle of a swamp. Tall, lush trees loom over a stone wall dripping moss down onto red and green tiles that weave into a mosaic pattern on the ground. Black, wrought iron benches, chairs and tables sit scattered around the patio. Some have tipped onto their sides. The algae and moss-covered stone fountain in the center is larger than it looks in photos. A mermaid sits atop a rock in its center holding a conch shell.

"Water would stream out from the shell," you say, pointing.

A yellow butterfly flutters between us and lights upon the edge of the fountain. We stay still, watching it tip-toe and flit its wings. When it launches back into the air, you brush off the spot where it had landed and gesture for me to take a seat. "That has to be some kind of sign," you say. "I have something. Don't move. I'll be right back."

I sit on the edge of the fountain and watch you dart back inside. You seem excited now. I'm not sure how I feel. I don't know if it's stupid to feel safe with you, to feel like what happened is okay because of how it's turning out.

You still drugged and kidnapped me, no matter the reason.

I should despise you, but I don't. You know the legend of Turtle Tear Island—you told me the story. You want to share this place with me. No, I don't despise you. I feel something entirely opposite, and I wish I didn't. You said it yourself—I'm a smart woman. I should know better.

You come back out onto the patio with a bottle of champagne in one hand and two chunky clay mugs in the other. You set the mugs on the ledge beside me and shake the champagne bottle. "Would you like to do the honors?" you ask, holding the bottle out to me.

I take it. "Aren't you afraid I'll point the cork at your face?"

You grin. "I deserve no less."

I press both thumbs on the cork and wiggle it out a bit before it pops and sprays champagne like my own conch shell fountain. You take it and pour us both a mugful.

"To Turtle Tear," you say, holding up your mug.

"To Turtle Tear." I hold mine up, and you tap yours against it.

We drink, eyeing each other over the rims of our mugs. Where do we stand? What happens now? Where do we go from here?

Four

You toss another log in the fireplace before striking a match and lighting the wadded up newspaper your using for kindling. Here in the lounge it's cool, unlike the stuffy attic bedroom.

The sun is setting. A blaze of gold and orange dapples through the tree leaves. A breeze blows through the open door behind me, and I pull the blanket you brought downstairs up around my shoulders and snuggle into my wrought iron chair from outside.

The champagne relaxed and warmed me a bit, but not enough to make it feel like I'm having an evening with a friend. I'm not sure there's enough champagne in the world for that.

"What are you thinking?" you ask. "You're so quiet." You refill your mug and offer the bottle to me.

I hold out my mug, and you top it off. "I'm wondering if anyone has ever been in a stranger situation."

You stare into the fire, considering. "Are you in love with me?"

"What? No! Why would you ask that?" I shift uncomfortably in my chair.

You smile and laugh to yourself. "Because that would

be a stranger situation, and it happens. Stockholm Syndrome. Women falling in love with their captors."

"I'm aware of what Stockholm Syndrome is." I take a deep drink, watching you smile like you know some secret that you aren't sharing.

"Be sure to let me know when that happens," you say.

"Don't count on it." You keep those deep, dark eyes on me with that cocky grin on your face. Your skin glows in the firelight. There's a shadow of stubble on your jaw and chin. I imagine it prickling against the delicate skin on my neck.

I rub my hand over my neck where it's flushing with heat and look away. "You're too used to getting everything you want."

"Maybe so." You tip your mug back and empty it then set it on the floor. "You look like you're freezing. Why don't you come down here in front of the fire?"

I cock an eyebrow. "Very smooth."

You hold your hands up and chuckle. "I won't try anything. If was going to, don't you think I had ample opportunity?"

I glance out the door behind me as another cool breeze blows over my shoulders and makes me shiver.

You pat the hardwood floor beside you. "Come on. Bring your blanket."

The fire cracks and pops, sparks fly up into the dark chimney. I sit, fold my legs to the side and lean my elbows on the hearth. I've always loved the smell of a wood fire burning, the way the smoke curls from the tongues of the tallest flames, the pounding heat on my face. "It feels nice."

"It is nice, isn't it?"

I feel your eyes on the side of my face. If I look at you, I'll be trapped in their depths.

I want to look.

I can't look. It's so wrong.

Thankfully, you lie back with your hands under your head, and I don't have to play tug-o-war with myself any longer.

"This reminds me of camping. I haven't been camping in probably twenty years." You roll onto your side and prop yourself up on your elbow. "My grandfather used to take my sister and me in his pop-up trailer."

My eyes dart to him. "A pop-up trailer? You?"

"I haven't always had money." You trace your finger along the seams between planks of wood on the floor. "Sometimes I'd trade it all to be that age again, to go camping and sit by a big fire roasting marshmallows without a care in the world." You frown and watch your finger on the floor. Your thick black eyelashes stroke your cheeks. "I'd do so many things differently."

I get the feeling you aren't just talking about what you did to me. I want you to keep talking, but I'm afraid if I ask, if I push, you'll stop. I sip champagne, watch you and wait for more words to fall from your lips.

You shift and your foot touches my leg. My instincts tell me to move away, but I don't want to.

"This," you say, gesturing all around us, "and you are my way of trying to make up for things in my past. I hope you understand I didn't ever want to hurt you. I didn't want to scare you. I just want to make things right."

"What are you trying to make right? You don't owe me anything. We have no past to fix." I don't want any more talk about righting wrongs or giving back to the universe. It's bullshit, and I know it. I want specifics. "Who did you wrong, Merrick? What happened?"

You stare into the fire for a few minutes, then fall back again with your eyes on the ceiling. My questions shut you down. You won't answer me.

A log falls off the stack in the fireplace. Sparks rain and embers glow dark red and bright yellow.

"Did you ever camp when you were young?" you ask.

"One time in sixth grade with the Girl Scouts. I like indoor plumbing and hate spiders. Once was enough."

The grin sneaks back onto your lips. You reach for me and make your fingers crawl up my thigh like a spider. I laugh because it tickles and jump back because you're touch on my bare skin feels way too good.

"I can open a bottle of wine if you want." Your expression is so warm and open. You're begging me to let my guard down—to let you in. I want to, but it's insane. You have issues, and I haven't gotten to the core of them yet.

"I don't think so."

Your smile slowly fades, and you nod. "Let me know if you change your mind."

"Okay." I smile because I don't want to hurt your feelings, and this realization makes me question my own sanity.

Maybe I need to stop thinking.

Your hair, your eyes, your smile and lips, that body . . . the pull is so strong. I can't deny how much I'm attracted to you, how I don't want to look away from your eyes, just gaze longer, harder, deeper until I'm completely inside you.

"What is it?" you whisper.

"You," I whisper back.

You hover closer. Flames reflect in your eyes. Inches stand between us. The warmth of your body—your lips, I want you. I need you.

I inhale sharply and turn away. "I think the fire needs stoked."

You sniff a few times and cough, recovering your self-control.

The best thing for me to do is go to sleep. I don't trust myself with you, and I don't want to regret anything in the light of day.

"I'll sleep down here," I say. "Unless you want to tie me back up?"

You toss another log on the fire and turn to me on your knees. "Of course not." You take my hand and squeeze. "You take the bed. I'll sleep down here, or on the couch upstairs."

I take my hand from yours. "Okay. I'm going to head up then." Before I let things between us get out of control.

You smile, understanding my unspoken reason for abruptly going to bed. "Sweet dreams, Rachael."

I gather the blanket and flee the room, dashing down the hall and up the arching staircase. I know my dreams will be of you, and I'm not sure how I'll stay away from you in the morning.

It's bright and birds are chirping like crazy feathered alarm clocks outside the window. It has to be early. It feels early.

I sit up in bed and rub my eyes. I didn't dream of you. I didn't dream at all.

My feet hit the hardwood floor with a thud, and I realize everything's different today. A thrill of anticipation runs up my back and down my arms. I wasn't kidnapped by a crazy man.

Okay, what you did was undeniably crazy, but also desperate and impulsive. There are deeper reasons behind your actions that I'm eager to uncover. Until I do, at least I know I'm in no danger, unless it's from my ever-increasing need to feel your lips on mine.

I shake my head to stem the flow of molten desire that takes over when I think of you. Today should be interesting.

Crossing the sitting area on my way to the bathroom, I stop when I notice you curled on your side on the couch. I had no idea you were there, sleeping silently. You're beautiful—it's the first thought that crashes through my mind. Men are rugged, handsome, athletic. You're all of these and more—you're a beautiful man.

I step closer running my eyes across your strong, shirtless back. The stubble on your face is darker, rougher. My fingers itch to touch it. I marvel at the angular shape of your face, your prominent cheekbones, thick-lashed, almond-shaped eyes, and how the dimple in your cheek dips in even while you sleep.

Your eyes flicker open. My heart jumps. You blink a few times while it sinks in that I'm standing above you staring. "Morning," you say, stretching and rubbing your eyes.

I should move away, stop staring, but I can't. "Morning."

You sit up and adjust your boxer shorts. I can't keep myself from peeking at the bulge pressing against the fly; the thin cotton barely contains you. My breath comes quicker, and I look away.

Dear God, I've never wanted someone so badly.

You stand and run your hands down each of my arms stealing my attention back. "I'm sorry you don't have any other clothes, but you can wear mine. Why don't you take a shower, and I'll lay something out for you?"

I step back and run into the coffee table. You pull me forward to keep me from falling, pressing me into your firm chest still warm from sleep. "Careful."

My nerves are quaking like some kind of freaked out animal. I tear myself away from you and stand a few feet away with my arms crossed over my chest. Confusion fogs your eyes. You have no idea what being so close to you does to me. "You can shower first," I say, grasping for words that make any sort of sense.

You stride to the dresser and pull open a drawer. "I

showered before bed." You glance back over your shoulder. "A cold shower." Those dark eyes hold mine, fill my mind with your meaning. You feel it, too—that raw ache that's planted itself deep down low in my belly that only wants one thing.

It feels like we're breathing the same breath in sync across the room, hearts drumming the same desperate, lonely beat. You turn away, and I inhale deeply, silently.

"There are clean towels in the linen closet in the bathroom." You pull a t-shirt from the drawer and toss it on the end of the bed.

"Thanks." I dart from the room into the hallway, my skin moist and tingling.

One look at the stairs at the end of the hall has me running through our conversation yesterday recalling your words—I'm the only one you could trust this place to. What did you hear in my voice that made you so certain I was the one you wanted here with you? What is it about you that makes me not want to leave?

It's more than this intense physical attraction. It's something I can't name. Something that feels like it runs through the earth. Something ancient and eternal. Something that's always been and always will be; bigger than both of us.

Maybe all your talk about bringing me here to right wrongs in the universe wasn't a bunch of bullshit. Somehow I think I know what you mean.

Hot water sings through the pipes and runs down my back. The shower is small and cramped, the tile is chipped like all the other tile in the hotel, but it's clean. Your shampoo smells exotic lathered in my hair, floral and spicy like jasmine and ginger. I rub my lips together; the cuts from trying to bite through the rope are almost healed. Thin lines of scabs circle both of my wrists, but aren't severe. There won't be scars. Soon there will be no evidence that you took me away and tied me to your bed. We'll be the only two people in the world who know—it'll only exist in our memories.

Should I let it go? Forget? Not speak a word of this to anyone?

I don't know.

A knock on the door startles me. I squeeze my arms over my breasts. "Rachael," you say, "come downstairs when you're dressed, okay?"

"Okay." You're right on the other side of the door. What would happen if you opened it?

So much. So much could happen if I let it.

I wait and listen, but you're gone.

Five

Your jogging shorts are big on me, but they have a drawstring that I pulled tight around my hips. The mesh material swings around my thighs like a skirt as I traipse down the stairs. The bottom of the sleeveless t-shirt you left on the bed for me is cut off. I saw a pair of scissors on top of the dresser, so I think you altered it so it wouldn't hang to my knees.

A bird perches in the broken window above the giant front doors. It warbles at me as I walk by crunching on broken glass in your borrowed flip-flops that are way too long and wide for my feet, but better than the platform heels I arrived wearing.

The scent of last night's fire lingers in the lounge. I find you out on the patio with coffee, fresh fruit and crusty bread. "I haven't seen a kitchen," I say, taking a seat beside you, "but you keep turning up with food."

You scoop pieces of cut-up fruit into a bowl and set it in front of me. "You don't need to be in a kitchen. I'll wait on you while you're here. You're my guest after all." You pour a cup of coffee and add two creams and one artificial sweetener, just like I like it.

"Did you make notes while you watched me at the

coffee shop?" I take the mug and sip. The hot coffee goes down like liquid Heaven.

Your neck flushes slightly, and your eyes fall to your lap. "No notes. I have a good memory."

You're punishing yourself with enough guilt that I feel terrible mentioning it. "Thank you." I pick up a piece of melon with my fingers and pop it into my mouth. Juice runs down my chin. There are no napkins, so I wipe furiously as I chew.

Your fingers join mine, wiping juice off my chin as you chuckle. "The watermelon's overly ripe. I should've warned you. And I couldn't find any napkins." You lick your fingers, and I imagine their sweet taste in my mouth as I suck the juice from them. My expression has to give me away, because you reach over and run your finger across my lips. When you take it away, I run my tongue over the same spot.

If you lean forward to kiss me right now, I won't stop you. If you keep going, keep touching me, I won't stop you.

"I won't..." You shake your head, reading my mind. "It has to be you."

The sun glints off your hair, riding the dark waves to your forehead. "What if I can't?" I ask. Making the first move has never been my strongpoint. I'm used to lusting at a distance and pining away unsatisfied until the guy loses interest. I always hold back. What if I give away what I'm feeling and get turned down? I don't set myself up for rejection. It's a fault of mine—I'm a successful overachiever because I don't take risks.

You shrug. Your lips quirk down. "Then you can't." You cut a slice of bread from the loaf and slather strawberry jam on it before handing it to me.

"How did all of this get here?" I ask, gesturing to the fruit, coffee, bread and jam. "If I'm here as a result of your desperate impulses, how is this place stocked with food?"

"I called my assistant on the way down." You pop a grape in your mouth and smile, proud of your ability to stock a kitchen on a moment's notice.

I do find it impressive. "So, I read one time that when you inherited Rocha Enterprises, it was only a handful of apartment units and one strip mall. Is that true? Did you make it what it is now?"

You sit back and take a sip of coffee, propping your foot up on your knee. "My grandpa left me the strip mall and my sister the three apartment buildings. My dad didn't want the hassle of rental properties. He was an accountant and had a job he was comfortable doing."

"Now you have an international enterprise worth billions of dollars." I can't help blinking when I look at you, thinking about your success, how brilliant you must be in business. It's like staring into a ball of fire. You intimidate me on so many levels.

You watch your finger flick a crumb of bread off the table. "Yeah, for all the good it does me."

You're the most tormented man I've ever met. "You don't enjoy your wealth?"

You turn your eyes on me. "I enjoy that it got me here

with you." You stand and sit your mug on the table. "Care for a tour of the island?"

Just when I'm starting to scratch the surface of your past, you change the subject. I take the last sip of coffee in my cup and reach for your hand. You watch our fingers interlace. It's a start and all I can manage for now. You squeeze tight and pull me up off my chair. "Watch where you step. There are snakes."

"Snakes?" These flip-flops don't seem like such a good idea anymore. Spiked heels would be much better for stepping on snakes.

"The island's wild. Nature's taken back over in the seventy-some years nobody's been here."

"There'll be spiders, too," I say, more to myself as a warning than to you.

You laugh. "I saw a big one inside this morning, but don't worry, I killed it."

My skin crawls, and I shiver. "Don't tell me that. I won't sleep tonight."

"You'll have a long night then. You'll need something to occupy your time." You open and close your hand around mine. I look at you out of the corner of my eye and see you smiling, waiting for my reaction.

"I'm sure I can find enough movies on T.V. to get me through until morning." I open and close my hand around yours, making you laugh.

"Ha. No movie channels. We barely get local stations. We're in the middle of nowhere if you haven't noticed." You tug me through the wrought iron gate and into an over-grown jungle of swamp grass, trees roots and vines that tug at my ankles. "We'll need to get a crew out here to clear most of the island. I was thinking we should leave the far eastern edge wild though. How does that sound?"

We'll need a crew? *We* should leave the eastern side wild? Who do you mean by we? "It's your island. Sounds good to me."

You press your lips together and exhale loudly out your nose. "If it's just mine..." You shake your head. "Like you said yesterday, a rundown hotel on a piece of land in the middle of the swamp does me no good. I'm not invested in this one to make a profit, Rachael. You love this place as much as I do, don't you?"

I glance back at the three-story, white, stucco hotel with its red tile roof and exposed rafter beams. The long windows are covered by black shudders propped open, looking like they're yawning, waking from a long sleep. "It's amazing. There's so much..." I can't find the right words. "It's alive."

I glance up at you, and the validation is written on your face. Validation for doing whatever you had to do to get me here with you—here at the hotel we both love that deserves nothing less than the two people who dream of bringing it to life again.

You close your eyes for a moment and slightly nod before tugging me along again through the tall grass. "So, we'll leave the eastern edge wild. A lot of the interior work we can do ourselves. Are you up for painting and helping me replace some windows?"

This has to be a test. Instead of approaching me from the standpoint of an employer offering a job, your new angle is to team up and make this a fun, friendly renovation. "Merrick, I can't stay. You know that."

Your arm circles my shoulders. "You can. I told you, I took care of everything."

"How did you take care of everything? What did you tell my mom? Shannon? I'm still finishing up an internship, you know."

Your chin jerks up in annoyance. "Internship. Please, Rachael, don't tell me you turned down my offer because of your internship. My assistant contacted your roommate and let her know you'd changed your mind about my offer and you're spending time in Florida to solidify your decision."

"Nice cover story. And what about my mom?" Irritation tangles with amusement inside me.

"Your mom's on an extended European cruise with your aunt. I talked to her personally. I let her know it was a perk for you joining me for a short time in Florida to consult on the Turtle Tear Hotel renovation."

"What?! She's on a cruise?" I yank your arm and make you face me. "What did you tell her, *exactly*?"

You smile with your entire face, reveling in my shock and laughing softly. "On our way down here, I had a nice talk with her. I told her it was last minute, that I escorted you down here, and I knew your concern for leaving her. I

asked if she would have anyone to join her on a vacation—
it was the least I could do for taking you away for a while."

I stand looking up at you, dumbfounded. "Everyone
knew I was coming here except me."

You tilt your head. "You were the last to know."

You did take care of everything. My mind is blank,
because I honestly have no idea what to make of all of this.
Nobody would be worried or looking for me. What if you
really had intended to hurt me? The sudden realization that
I was taken away so easily sends waves of panic from my
back to my chest. I try to tell myself to be calm. I'm not in
danger. Don't think of what could have been.

"What are you thinking?" you ask.

I throw my hands in the air. "I have no idea what to
think."

"Then don't." You hook your arm through mine and we
begin walking again. "I'll show you where the helicopter
lands."

Everything about the past few days is surreal.

I'm here with you, Merrick Rocha, on Turtle Tear Island.

My mom is on a European cruise that you sent her on.

I have a happy mom on a dream cruise, my dream hotel
renovation and you...my dream man? I'm not certain, but I
think I would feel that way if I let myself forgive you.

Six

We stand in the center of a clearing beside a black helicopter. The tall grass around us has been blown over. It lies flat on the ground. "It's the only spot on the island where there are no trees. I was afraid it might be a marsh when I first landed the helicopter here."

"When was that? How many times have you been here?"

You pat the side of the helicopter and lean against it. "About two years ago. This is my third time."

Third time's a charm. Funny, I've only slept with my high school boyfriend and my ex-boyfriend, Lance, who I met my second year in college and dated for two years—you'd be my third. Experience isn't on my side.

I run my eyes up your strong legs, over the lines of your chest where your t-shirt hugs, down your well-defined arms—I can't imagine how good they would feel wrapped around me.

I want you to be my third. If I get the courage to make a move, I have to be sure it's more than just sex. I'm not a one-time and done kind of girl. I'd be crushed if I got past how we started and gave myself to you only for it never to happen again—if that was all you wanted.

"The island's three miles in circumference, right?" I need to get my mind off of you and me and all that implies.

"It is." You step toward me and hold out your hand. "I've never been all the way around. Let's go explore."

There are a lot of things on this island I'd like to explore.

My fingers tingle as I take your hand. We head to the far side of the clearing and duck into the trees. "Whoa. How are we getting through here?" Mangrove roots arch and turn, forming cage-like structures at the base of each tree.

"We climb and watch for water. I don't want you sinking." Your hand slips up my arm and clamps down just above my elbow. "Hold tight."

I twist my fingers in the side of your t-shirt and follow you, stepping where you step. You help me up and over the mangrove roots. It takes us a while, but finally, we emerge from the tangled trees into tall grass that gives way to a sea of water lilies.

"There's water under there," you say, pointing to the lilies. You grip me even tighter. "I don't want to scare you, but watch for gators. You never know."

My eyes skirt around us, delving into the tall grass and lilies. "Maybe we should go back."

"Look over there," you say, ignoring my suggestion. "It's a boat house."

The ramshackle wooden structure looks like an abandoned shack to me, not a boathouse, but I step lightly behind you through slick mud, admittedly curious about what's inside.

Bugs buzz in the trees, and the relentless sun beats down on my face. It has to be nearing noon. I slip; one foot shoots out from under me. You lunge for me and pull me against you before I fall.

"Thanks." I'm pressed into you, your hands flat on my back holding me tight. Your eyes are hazy, expectant.

I reach up—my hand shakes—and brush a curl back from your forehead. I caress your cheek with my eyes; run them over your nose and down to your lips. Should I?

In my hesitation, you to set me back on my feet before I have a chance to act. "Close one," you mutter. I'm not sure if you mean my slip, or the almost kiss.

You forge ahead the few yards to the boathouse and peer inside. "Hey! Looks like we're catching our dinner."

I catch up and find you digging around through fishing gear inside a big canoe. "I thought you said the kitchen was stocked."

"We're on an island!" You're beaming holding a net in one hand and a fishing rod in the other. "Let's get out on the water and see what we can catch."

I can't help but laugh at your exuberance. A flash of what you were like as a young boy comes to mind. All curls and big brown eyes. "Did you go fishing with your grandpa when you went camping?" I step in the canoe beside you and pick up a red and white bobber.

"Yeah," you say bending and opening a tackle box. "My sister was like the fish whisperer. Every time her bait hit the water a fish would jump on." You take a rusty hook out of the box and hold it up examining it.

"You weren't as lucky?" I toss the bobber up and catch it.

You chuckle. "I have crap luck at fishing. Let's hope you're better."

"Don't count on it. Thank God for grocery shopping assistants, huh?"

Your wide grin mesmerizes me. You narrow your eyes, holding a question in them.

I lift my brows. "What?"

"I hoped I could make you happy by bringing you here. I guess I never realized that I'd get something from you."

Now I narrow my eyes at you. "What are you getting from me?"

"I haven't smiled this much in a long, long time."

"And I haven't even kissed you yet." The words slip out before I realize what I'm saying. My eyes widen, and I suck in my lips.

You laugh and pull me in for a hug. "I'm glad it's on your mind at least. I've been dying to know what's been going on in there." You playfully tap your knuckles on top of my head.

"Glad I gave that away," I mumble, making you laugh louder.

Out on the water, you cast your line with a shiny fake bug on the hook for bait. The boat rocks, and I grab the sides. You watch me, relaxed and amused.

Fortunately, we only found one reel, so I'm off the hook for the fishing part of this expedition. Instead, I slip to the bottom of the boat and stretch my arms and legs out in the sun hoping I don't burn to a crisp. Water laps at the sides of the boat. A fish jumps. Birds fly high overhead calling to each other.

"Content?" You balance the pole against your bench and lean back to wait for a bite.

"Why would you say that?" I can't give you satisfaction for dragging me here yet.

You fold your arms over your chest and quirk a smile. "You sighed."

"Could've been a sigh of irritation." I glance away from you then back. I can't stop looking.

Your dimples deepen. "No, it was contentment." You mimic my sigh and thread your fingers behind your head. "I could live here. Maybe I won't leave."

"Don't you have responsibilities? A little business to run?" I nudge your leg with my bare foot.

Your gaze shifts out over the water. "I've been thinking about retiring."

"You're thirty-two!"

"I'm a billionaire." You sit forward and pick up your rod, reel in the line and cast it back out. "None of it matters, anyway. What does it mean to own a bunch of buildings?"

"You're not old enough to have a mid-life crisis, you know." I nudge you again, but you don't respond. "It has whatever meaning you give it."

You rub the stubble on your jaw. "Yeah. I guess that's the problem. It doesn't mean much anymore. It's just...empty.

I don't know. It doesn't make me happy anymore. Maybe it never did."

"This place makes you happy, so you're ready to chuck it all in for a rundown hotel and a canoe?"

You close your eyes and nod. "I don't want the competition anymore, the back-stabbing, the rumors. It's so peaceful here without all of that."

What's happened to you to make you want to throw it all away? "It's a big decision." Your whole life has had to have been wrapped up in your business to make it what it is today.

Your eyes open, and you lean toward me. "That's another reason I had to have you here. You know how to make hard decisions—even ones that tear you up inside, like turning down a job you really want. I need you to help me make mine."

I rise back up on my bench so we're eye-to-eye. "I can't help you make that decision, Merrick. I barely know you."

You take a strand of my hair and pluck out a leaf. Our hair and eye coloring are so similar; we could be brother and sister. Only the heat I feel at your touch isn't sisterly at all. "We've only just started our time here together," you say, flicking the leaf in the water. "You'll know me well enough soon."

"How long will I be here?" You make it sound like this is an extended stay for both of us.

"A few weeks." You lean back again and pick up your pole. "This time."

"I can't..." Before I finish saying I can't stay, I realize that I can. I'm not missing anything at home. My internship—my internship sucked anyway. I haven't found a job yet after turning you down.

You eye me across the boat. "You can. I made sure of it."

I've never been free to do whatever I want. From the time I was old enough to take the dance classes my mom signed me up for, through college at the university she and dad chose— close to home—through the past few years trying to intern and help my mom care for my dad after his cancer diagnosis. Then he passed away and she was so lonely. I couldn't leave her. My time, my choices have never been my own.

"Do you resent having to answer to everyone else?" You're staring at me, very perceptive of my feelings. Too perceptive.

"Sometimes. Then I feel guilty." Your bobber dips underwater and pops back up. I smack your leg and point. "You got one!"

"No way." You jerk the line and start reeling it in. "I never catch anything. You must be my lucky charm." You wink at me and pull an ugly green-brown fish out of the water. "Big mouth bass."

I grab the net and hold it out for you. Once the fish is in the boat, you take the hook out and plop him in a rusty bucket with some lake water. "You're keeping it?" It stares up at me with a big, googly eye, its gills flaring.

"I told you, we're eating it tonight." Your head joins mine over the bucket. "Mmm, mmm. Good eatin'."

Laughter erupts from my belly. "Are you sure you're a billionaire business god?"

Your laughter joins mine. "I did sound like I real swamp-man just then, didn't I?"

"If you do stay here, you'll fit in nicely with the neighbors." I put a hand up, shading my eyes. "If there are any in a hundred mile radius." I drop my hand and shrug. "You can always fly them in."

"Nah. Too pretentious. I'll stick with the canoe." You sit and cast the line back out. "Let's see if your luck holds."

Turning on my bench, I glance out across the water, scanning in all directions. There is so much untamed green—trees, lilies, sea grass—it's like we're pioneers who trekked out here and discovered this secluded spot.

A firefly wisps by my head, hovers like a helicopter between us, then darts away. How can you mesh your life of luxury with one on a deserted island?

You reel the line in a little and prop your foot up on the side of the boat. Every wall that stood between us before has vanished. You're still a stranger, but at the same time, you're not, and my curiosity is getting the better of me. "Tell me more about yourself. All I know is the business side from interviews in magazines and online articles. I don't know anything about you as a person."

"Want to get personal, huh?" Your eyes sparkle with light reflecting off the water. The look in them clearly shows me how personal you'd like to get. "What do you want to know?"

"What about your sister? How old is she? What's her name? Do you have any other siblings?" The questions burst out of me. For a second, my eagerness embarrasses me, and I take another glimpse of our surroundings to pull my eyes from yours.

"Her name's Heidi. She's three years younger than me, and no, I don't have any other siblings."

I face you again and lift my brows, encouraging you to keep talking.

You tilt your head and almost smile. "Nobody ever asks about my family. All I am is a figure in a bank account or a signature on a paycheck." Leaning forward, you run your hand down my arm. "Thank you for asking."

I can't figure out if this is another one of your attempts at changing the topic, but I won't let you this time. "Do you get along with her? Heidi?"

You sit back and rub your hands on your shorts. "We get along. We don't talk much."

"Why?" You run a hand through your hair. My questions make you nervous. "You don't like talking about yourself, do you?" I ask.

Leaning your elbows on your knees, you gaze at me, resignation crossing your eyes. "I'm not used to it, but I will. For you, I will." Your throat ripples as you swallow. "Heidi's husband and I don't get along. He doesn't think I'm a good influence, so she doesn't contact me very often."

"Why does he think that way? Did something happen?" Does he know you drug and kidnap woman, take them to an island and wine and dine them, offer them everything they've ever wanted?

I blink and keep my eyes closed for a second to stop the swirling mix of thoughts and emotions in my head.

"Nothing really happened. She got married, and after they had my niece and nephew, he thought I was pushing my work ethic onto Heidi every time I called to discuss business or ask her to travel to one of our properties away from home. Eventually, she left the business. She still has the three apartment buildings our grandpa left her, and I bought out her percentage of ownership of the business. Now we only talk on holidays."

"That seems extreme." Growing up an only child, I can't imagine how great it would be to have a brother or sister. Nothing would keep me from having a relationship with them.

You watch your foot slide back and forth in a puddle of water in the bottom of the boat. "My brother-in-law told me I was hurting her, that my expectations were too high and she felt like she was always letting me down. He said I didn't have any obligations, like a wife and kids, so I didn't understand what I was putting her through."

Your eyes meet mine, and there's so much pain in them, they make my chest ache.

"He said," you continue, "I keep taking and taking from her, but never give back. She needed me to give her understanding and patience. I didn't know how. I lost her."

"You didn't lose her," I say without thinking. There's no way for me to know if you have or not.

Sitting up and taking a deep breath, you take the fishing rod and reel the line in a little. "What other questions do you have for me?"

I'm almost afraid to ask, but if you're inviting transparency, then I'm not backing off. "You've never mentioned your mom."

"She died when I was seven. Cancer." You reel the line in a little more.

After my dad's year-long battle with cancer, I know all about losing someone you love to that evil monster. "I'm sorry. You were so young to lose her."

Your shoulders quirk, not quite a shrug. I can't let you bottle up again.

"What was she like?"

Your throat contracts again as you swallow. My questions aren't getting easier for you to answer. "She was fun. She laughed a lot. She always smelled like the lilacs that grew outside my bedroom window." You blink a few times, and your eyes are misty. "She always said I gave the best hugs."

I have the sudden urge to know all about those hugs—to comfort you. "She sounds like a great mom."

"Yeah," you sigh and tug the line. "What else?"

"Is your father still alive?" Might as well keep diving straight into the deep water.

"Oh, he's alive all right. He's suing me for what he claims is his right to a percentage of the business he was too busy to take over from my grandpa."

I can't believe my ears. "Your father is suing you?" It's incredible—unimaginable.

"Has been for years. I refuse to settle, and he refuses to give up."

"That's insane."

"I'm glad someone sees my side." You jerk the line and start reeling fast. "Got another one. You truly are lucky."

Watching your arms flex as you land the fish, I can't help but wonder what your relationships with your family have done to you. Are you simply misunderstood? Lonely? Hurting? "Have you tried to make things better with your dad or Heidi?"

You gesture to the net, and I pick it up to help. "I don't know how to make things better, Rachael."

"Maybe I can…" What am I offering? To be your friend? Why? I don't owe you anything but animosity. "Maybe I can help you figure it out." It's too late to turn back. I can't help how I feel, even if my brain is telling me I'm stupid for feeling this way.

You freeze with the fish in your hand and study my face. You're as surprised by my offer as I am. "I'd like that."

For a moment my heart speeds with the strong pull between us, but I nudge your hand with the net and your attention finds its way back to the fish on your line.

I'm treading in emotional quicksand with you—up to my knees with no way out.

Paddling back to the boathouse, the sky grows dark and sheets of rain race toward us across the water. "We're going to get wet," you say.

Lightening slices the sky. A crack of thunder makes me jump. "I hate storms."

"We'll be off the lake soon." I watch you paddle, wishing there was another so I could help us get back faster.

The wind blows so hard, trees bend. Another flash of lightening blinds the sky, and thunder rumbles overtop of us. A loud mechanical noise hums and echoes. "What's that?"

"Backup generator." Your chest flexes and contracts with each stroke. Taking you in, my fear is instantly replaced with a rush of desire only to be yanked back by another jolt of lightening.

We hit the shore. You grab the bucket of fish, rod and tackle box. I hop out of the canoe and run as fast as I can for the boathouse.

Inside, it's dark and musty. We pant, catching our breath. "Guess we wait it out in here," you say, hauling the fish to a small wooden table underneath a window in the back. "Wonder if I can find a knife in here to clean these."

You search shelves and corners while I dig through the

tackle box, finally coming up with a small paring knife. "Will this work?" I hold it up for you to see.

"Perfect." Your fingers run over mine when you take it from me. My stomach tightens, my skin prickles. My body responds to your touch more than I want it to.

From behind, I watch you clean fish in silhouette, blocking most of the dim light streaming in the window. A loud crash of thunder has me taking a few strides closer to you.

"It's okay," you say, looking at me over your shoulder. "This place has been here a long time. I doubt that this is the day it'll fall down around us."

"I hope not." But now that you've put the thought into my head, it's the only thing I can think of. "How would we know if this was a hurricane?"

You filet one of the fish and toss the bones aside. "It's not a hurricane. Just a storm. It'll pass." After setting the knife on the table, you hold your hands out. "I don't have a towel or anything. Guess I should've thought about this before getting my hands covered with fish guts." With a quick swoop over your head, your chest is bare and you're wiping your hands on your t-shirt.

Lightning flashes on your skin through the window making you look like Adonis—or Zeus with his lightning bolts, but not simply a man. Your tan shorts hang low on your hips, your six-pack abs lead to a defined V like an arrow to follow down past your fly where my eyes can't follow. But they want to. They so want to.

"We need to make a run for it," I say. You have to get a shirt on that body before I lose all control.

You chuckle. "A minute ago you were afraid we were stuck in a hurricane. Now you want to run out in the middle of it?"

I hold up a finger and watch the window. "Wait. Let's see how far away the storm is now." When the lightning flashes again, I start counting. "One, one-thousand, two, one- thousand—"

"What are you doing?" You look at me like I'm a circus act.

"Shh. Three, one-thousand, four, one-thousand, five—" Thunder rumbles. "It's one mile away. We can make it."

You glance at the window, then back at me. "What did you just do?"

"You count the seconds between the lightning and thunder then divide by five. That's the distance to the storm. You've never heard of this?"

One side of your mouth twists up, revealing a dimple. "Never. Must be something you learned at Girl Scout camp that one time." You dip your shirt into the bucket of lake water where you'd stashed the fish in the boat. When it's soaking wet, you wrap the filets in it. "Let's run for it then. Want to race?"

You dart by me and out the door, your laughter drowning in the distant thunder. I sprint after you, rain pelting down on us soaking our clothes and hair. You look back over your shoulder, then slow and turn around, jogging backward. "Come on slow poke!"

If I wasn't afraid of stepping on a snake or cutting my foot on a sharp rock, I'd take your flip-flops off and throw them at you. Lightning streaks across the sky, jutting down into a tree across the island. Thunder rips through the sky and shakes the ground. I cry out and curse under my breath, calling you every name I can think of.

You run back to me. "I think your counting may have been off. This storm is right on top of us. Hop on." You turn around and bend down for me to climb on your back. I do, without hesitation and bury my face into your neck. I don't want to see or hear the storm for one more second. We could be struck down right here in the tall grass and mud and nobody would ever find us.

"Hurry," I whisper, clutching your shoulders so tight my fingers are numb.

I close my eyes and bounce up and down on your back as you run. Your fingers clutch my thighs, holding me tight to your body. I won't let myself think about how good it feels to cling to you, to wrap my legs around you and have your hands on me.

I focus on the sound of your feet pounding on the ground, the rain blowing down and the thunder. Suddenly, it seems like a good idea if it stormed all night. God knows I'm going to need a distraction if tonight is anything like last night.

Seven

"This is the kitchen?" My eyes can't take it all in. While parts are still in ruins, like the crumbling marble countertop on the far wall and the rotting wooden butcher-block island, other features are updated. A new six burner gas range has been installed along with an enormous stainless steel refrigerator.

You stand at a deep, white farmhouse-style sink that has to be original to the hotel, rinsing the fish you've unwrapped from your t-shirt. "I made some improvements." You gesture to the range and the fridge. "If you don't like them, they can be changed. They're here for our convenience, not necessarily to stay."

Our convenience. Another word joining us together—we, us, our. I'm getting used to how it sounds. Is that a good thing, or a bad thing? I need to decide before turning back isn't an option.

"Why don't you go up and change out of those wet clothes while I get dinner started?" You reach over and tug on your white t-shirt that's soaked and clinging to me revealing the chill that's seeped into my skin making the tips of my breasts stand erect. Your eyes fall to my chest and don't waver. Your hand contracts tighter around the t-shirt, pulling me closer.

I can almost feel your touch where your eyes linger. It makes my nipples even harder. I'm losing myself to you. Your thumb strokes against the bare flesh on my stomach, making my back arch toward you. I gasp, pull the shirt out of your hand and spin around. "Okay."

I can't even think as I dash through the pool of standing water in the entryway that flooded in through the broken window. My mind races in dizzying circles. Want and need battle with the insane circumstances of us being together on this island in the first place. How can I possibly give in to that? How do I forgive you? I want to—I run my hands over my stomach, up to my chest, over my nipples aching for your fingers, your mouth—God, I want to.

This is dangerous. *You're* dangerous. You can't just take whatever you want—that includes me. You seem to know that though, that I'm off limits until I give myself to you. You don't want to take me—at least not that way, not intimately.

My body and mind are so conflicted it makes me crazy. My body screams for me to give in—I'm here on this island in this amazing historic hotel where I've dreamed of being, alone with a man who I am so attracted to I could explode on contact. I can't even imagine how incredible sex would be with you. Thinking about it makes me tingle and ache, makes my mouth water, eager to taste you.

But my head…my head can't wrap around the idea of giving myself to a man who had zero consideration for my own free will—a man who can't communicate what he wants, so he takes it because he's powerful and controlling and nobody stops him from getting what he wants.

You wanted me.

You wanted me so badly you went to desperate ends, risking everything to have me. That makes me so hot; I have to grip the railing tighter to keep myself from running back into the kitchen and pulling your clothes off—giving myself to you on the kitchen floor.

You don't seem like a monster, but are you? Do I even care anymore, or has my burning body won out already?

When I come down from my shower, wearing a pair of your boxer shorts and another of your t-shirts, the aroma wafting from the kitchen is amazing. My stomach grumbles.

I find you in the lounge building a fire like last night. An open wine bottle and our two mugs sit on the hearth. "Better?" you ask, smiling as I approach.

"Much. I'll watch dinner while you go up if you want."

"No need. It's done. I'm keeping it warm." You pour wine into a mug and hand it to me. "I'll be quick. I don't know about you, but I'm starving."

"I am too. It smells fantastic. Where did you learn to cook?" I sip the wine, a fruity, dry white, light and crisp on my tongue.

"I've always cooked. After my mom died, my dad buried himself in work and spent most of his time closed up in his office. Heidi hated cooking and I hated doing laundry, so we split the chores."

"You were so young. I don't think I was even allowed

to use the stove until I was a teen." The more I learn about you, the more I understand why you are how you are. Never having been given anything, no wonder you grew up to become a man who takes anything he can get.

"It was cook or starve." You chuckle, oblivious to the fact that your statement sends a pang of sadness through me. "I'll hurry."

I want to run after you, hold you, comfort you, take care of you. I don't think anyone ever has. How can a gorgeous, wealthy man be so alone?

With emotions taking over my body and mind, I drink deeply from my mug and pour myself another full cup of wine. To hell with it—I'm throwing caution to the wind, letting the chips fall where they may, all of those sayings apply tonight. I can't help that I want you. All I can do is go with it and see where we end up.

I drain the second mug of wine and pour another. By the time you come back to the lounge, I'm warm from the alcohol and the fire, and only slightly nervous with anticipation of what tonight holds for us.

"Wow." You lean over me and pick up the mostly empty wine bottle on the hearth. "You were thirsty." Your eyes are soft and warm, luring me in. My nose picks up the scent of your spicy, exotic, jasmine shampoo and the fresh, clean smell of soap. But there's also a distinctly masculine scent mingling with the others. I resist the urge to lean into your shoulder and breathe you in. "What?" Your eyes narrow. "You look…"

I look turned on. I am turned on. You've been so perceptive of my feelings, you have to know.

A faint smile crosses your lips and you close your eyes for a moment. "I'll get dinner." You stand and pour the rest of the wine in my mug. "And another bottle."

"I'll help." Before I can stand, you run your hand down the side of my head, stroking my hair.

"No. You stay. Let me serve you." The tip of your finger brushes my cheek, lighting my skin with a fiery trail of tingles.

You return a few minutes later with two plates filled with fish, rice and a mixed greens salad. "Thank you." I take my plate and keep my eyes on you as you lower yourself beside me. We're so close, our legs almost touch.

"I hope you like it." You pour yourself a mug of wine and hold it up to mine. "To…" your eyes cling to mine, "us…tonight, here, with you."

My breath comes slow and deep, the wine lingers in my head, your words flow inside me. *Us. Tonight. Here.* Yes, I want that.

You break a piece of flaky fish off with your fork and hold it out to me. "Try it. Let me know if I've done it how you like it."

Every word you speak has a double meaning in my mind. My insides are molten, melted, gushing. I open my mouth, and you slide your fork inside. I close my lips around the tines and let my eyes fall shut savoring the taste—buttery, lemony, lightly seasoned. "Mmm…"

You slide the fork out between my lips, and I open my eyes, meeting your intense gaze. "You keep that up and I'll be feeding you every bite of food you ever take." Your voice is husky. You're barely holding back.

I grasp your wrist and take the fork. "You tell me how good it is." I offer you a piece of fish. You open your lips and touch it with your tongue before sliding it off with your teeth.

Every part of my body becomes hyper aware of you. Nerve endings crawl to the surface and prickle in antici-pation.

"It's good, but it's not what I'm hungry for." You grab the fork from my hand and toss it on the hearth. Leaning into my ear, your voice comes out in a growl. "I'd like to show you how big my appetite is."

My chest heaves. My heart pounds. Your warm breath sends tingles down my spine. I can't take it anymore and turn my head toward yours. My nose brushes down your stubbly jawline. You tilt your face so our lips are almost touching.

My inhales are your exhales; we share mingled breaths. I lick my lips. A hard sigh rasps out of you. You want this. "Let me..." you whisper.

My lips itch for yours. I lift my chin and they barely touch. Soft. Warm. We linger like that for endless seconds, until we're both panting for more. My tongue sneaks out and glides along your bottom lip. It's all it takes for you to come undone.

You clutch my chin and pull my mouth against yours. Your tongue sweeps against mine, stroking and plunging, stoking the heat in my core. Mindless from wine and desire, I push you onto your back, our lips never parting, and lie on top of you. Our kisses are urgent, our breath heaving and panting. Between my legs, I'm damp and pulsing with need.

You take my face between your hands and pull our lips apart to look in my eyes. "I'm not instigating anything, Rachael. You touch me, then I touch you. It has to be you first. You're in control. If you want me, you can take me."

Take this man, this body, these lips and hands. I want you all over me. I want to take you to the edge and then push you to explode. I dive back into your lips, let my knees fall to the sides of you and rock my hips against yours. Your erection is hard and long, rigid against your shorts. You rise up to meet me, and we fall into a frantic rhythm, grinding against each other.

"Take me, Rachael." You groan and raise your hands over your head, clutching the air. "God, I want to feel you."

I grab your wrists and pin them over your head. Rising up on my arms, I drown in the lust in your eyes while I ride you. I've never taken control like this before, and nothing has ever felt so intense. You've awoken a side of me I didn't know existed. "What do you want to touch, Merrick?"

Saying your name sends a wave of longing through me like I've never known. I dip my head and lick your full, amazing lips. "Fuck," you mutter. "I want to squeeze those hard little nipples. Tear my boxers off of you and shove my fingers into the wetness between your legs."

I rub against your faster, moaning. I'm so ready I can't stand it.

The memory of waking up tied to the bed flashes through my mind. Fear and desperation jolt through me. I dart away from you, gasping for breath. "I can't." I jump up, tearing my hands through my hair. "I can't."

I take off down the hall toward the stairs ignoring you calling my name, ignore the sound of a mug shattering against the fireplace.

In your bedroom, I run through the sitting area and crawl into bed. Tears come hot and fast down my cheeks. The need and want are still raw inside me, but my mind won't let them win, not even when numbed by wine.

I roll onto my back and grip the sheets, willing the heat to leave my body. I can't take you. I can't have you. Not now—maybe never. I hate myself for not letting go. Why do I always have to do the sensible and logical thing? For once, I just wanted to take what I need.

After an hour of crying and rolling from side to side, I still can't get rid of the ache between my legs. I need release and have to give it to myself.

I slip my hand inside your boxers and spread my legs, sighing at the wetness my fingers find. I'm dripping. If only I could let you slide inside me and give me the relief I crave. I stroke the fleshy, sensitive tip in circles, knowing I'm going over the edge fast.

My fingers slide down the middle, and I raise my knees up, pushing two fingers inside. My other hand slips under your t-shirt and tugs the nipple you wanted so badly to squeeze.

"Rachael…"

I gasp, pull my knees together and curl into a ball. You're leaning against the wall in the dark between the sitting area and the bed. Moonlight streaming in the window beside me caresses your body. You've taken your shirt off. Your chest is bare, your fingers run over your abs down to your waistband as you take me in.

"Don't stop," you say, pleading, desperate. "You're so beautiful." You unbutton and unzip your shorts. Your hard, long erection leans toward me. "I'll stay right here. Please don't stop." You wrap your hand around your wide base and begin to stroke up and down your length. Your head falls back, but your eyes bore into mine. "I won't touch you."

So close to the edge before you came in, I'm ready to come just watching you. If I touch myself, I won't be able to hold back.

I spread my legs and squeeze my breasts, rub my nipples. You dig your teeth into your bottom lip and suck in a deep breath. "So fucking sexy." You stroke faster and harder.

I want to make you come so bad. I push my shirt up so you can see my full, aroused breasts, lick my fingertips and rub them in tiny circles over my hard nipples. You groan and pound your fist against the wall. "You're killing me," you growl.

I haven't punished you nearly enough. My hand slides back down between my legs. "Let me see," you whisper. "Please. Let me see." You hold up your free hand. "No touching."

I swallow hard, passion and desire consuming me, and slide the boxers off.

"*Ah*, shit." You knock your head against the wall behind you, your hand still wrapped tight, jerking and sliding up and down your considerable length.

My fingers circle my swollen clit and glide down my middle. My knees fall apart wider, my hips rock. I tremble and moan and plunge my fingers inside. Finding the spot I know will make me lose my mind. I rub harder, pushing in and pulling out faster.

"Come with me. I'm so close." Your words are a husky rasp.

Flames ignite up my thighs, pulling them apart even farther, make my hips quake and my back arch. "Oh, God, yes!" I cry, throwing my head back into the pillow, enjoying the throbbing around my fingers, relief flowing over me like warm water.

"Ah, shit. Rachael, "You gasp and groan. I watch you stroke your tip lightning fast, come erupting out of you. You shudder, find my eyes and slide down the wall, spent, panting. I want to touch you so badly it hurts. "Thank you," you whisper.

"How long were you standing there?" The thought of

you watching without my knowing simultaneously excites and terrifies me.

"I said your name as soon as I saw what you were doing. I wouldn't...do that. I told you I respect your privacy—always have." You stand and clean up with your discarded t-shirt before fastening your shorts and lying on the couch, your head at the far end so you can see me.

I roll to my side and let myself get lost in your gaze. Neither of us says a word; we just appraise each other for the longest time. "You're so beautiful and sexy," you finally say. "I'll never forget that."

"Neither will I." The vision of him pleasuring his incredible body while watching me sends pulses of heat between my legs. If I don't stop thinking about it soon, we might have to have a repeat session.

You yawn, roll onto your side and curl your knees up. "Goodnight, sweet Rachael."

"Sweet dreams," I whisper.

You let out a low, guttural chuckle. "There won't be anything sweet about the dreams I'm about to have. *Stimulating*, yes. Sweet, no."

I smile into the pillow knowing I did this to you, and I'll do it again.

The next morning I wake to a single yellow calla lily laying on the nightstand on top of a note written in scrawled, manly handwriting. With the flower in one hand, I hold the paper in the other.

> This reminded me of you and last night. Beautiful with soft pedals leading into dark places I can only hope to touch.
>
> —M

The lily's pedals fold back revealing a deep, dark, narrow cup where the flower meets the stem. It does resemble a certain part of the female anatomy. The gesture is sensual and full of meaning. I run the flower across my cheek smiling and flushing from head to toe. Never have I had the courage to touch myself in front of a man before... before you.

Another yellow calla lily lies at the bottom of the stairs on the floor in the entryway. I pick it up, and my eyes fall on yet another under the archway leading into the hall. One after another, they lead me through the lounge, out onto the patio and through the wrought iron gate.

The hot sun beats down on the ground still damp from yesterday's storm making the day hazy and humid. Birds chortle and chirp in the tangle of trees and flowering vines. The air smells like honeysuckle and rain. Another flower lies on a chunk of broken pebble sidewalk that used to form a path to wherever you're leading me.

I weave through the trees collecting my lilies. Up ahead, there's a cloister—thick wooden beams and white stucco supporting the same red-tiled roof as the hotel. Underneath, you lounge in a rope hammock watching me. "Morning," you call out. "You found me."

I hold up the lilies. "It was hard not to." I make my way over to you. The covered walkway encloses a square court-yard with a pool in ruins in the center. Palm trees tower over the rubble from each of its corners. Tiny multi-colored tiles that once lined the pool lie scattered and broken in the grass and piled in the bottom.

"Wow," I say. "It's beautiful even in ruins."

"It is beautiful." You hook your finger around mine. You're looking at me though, not the courtyard. "I have something for you." You reach down beside you and hold up my wristlet—the one I had at the club the night you took me. "I charged your phone if you want to make a call."

My fingers wrap around the wristlet, and I clutch it to my chest. You trust me to have my phone? "Aren't you afraid of who I'll call?" What if I call the police?

You sit up, your chest still bare from last night, and train your despondent eyes on mine. "After last night…" A heavy sigh passes between your lips. "I can't make you trust me. I know what I've done to you. You either do or you don't."

"That's a lot to ask someone you've only known a few days." I lower onto the hammock beside you, sliding down into the center, our shoulders and thighs press together tight.

"It's been…" You reach up and brush a piece of hair off my face, tucking it behind my ear. "An intense few days." You put an arm around my waist. "Here, lean back and look up."

I let you pull me down beside you so my head rests on your warm shoulder. "What am I supposed to be looking at?" My eyes follow your finger, pointed up to the top of one of the wooden beams supporting the roof.

"Do you see those initials up there, A.W. plus I.B. with a heart around it?"

I squint and tilt my head toward yours a little.

Your nose glides across my cheek and up through my hair over my ear. "Does the name Archibald Weston ring any bells?"

"Oh my God. Archibald and Ingrid." I fight the distraction of your warm breath on my neck.

Your finger loops through my hair; your nose nuzzles my ear. "Somebody once told me a story of a man who went to great lengths to get the woman he wanted here on this island. He whisked her away, and she never wanted to leave."

I gaze up at the initials etched into the almost century old wood. "That's where you got the idea? I gave it to you?"

"You may have planted the seed." Your chuckle sparks goose bumps over my chest and down across my stomach. Your finger traces from my temple down to my chin. "If I offered to take you home, would you stay anyway, Rachael? Just for a little while longer?"

My conflicted mind starts pushing and pulling, emotion, passion and desire pitted firmly against logic, reason and morals. "Don't offer. I don't want to have to think about it."

"I think maybe you have," you whisper, "and that's why

you don't want me to offer. You're afraid you'll stay here with me."

I place a finger over your lips. "Shh. Don't. It makes my head hurt thinking about it."

Your tongue traces my fingertip before you take my hand away and hold it in yours. "Are you hungry? You have to be. We didn't eat much dinner before things, um, took a turn last night."

"Strangely, I'm not. I think I had too much wine. My stomach's a little queasy."

You dangle your leg over the side of the hammock and nudge your toes on the patio, rocking us gently. "I like my boxers on you." *And off of you,* lingers unspoken between us.

"What's your timeline for the hotel renovation?" I have to stop this steam train before it derails me again.

You kiss my knuckles before answering. "That's up to you."

"I'm not the project manager, remember?"

"You can call yourself whatever you want to, but you're here now. I told you this place is yours." Your dark eyes flicker up to the initials carved on the wooden beam, leaving my heart to beat wildly in speculation of what's running through your mind. "Yours to do whatever you want with." Your hand holds mine firmly against your chest, directly over your heart.

"Merrick..." I don't know what to say. "I don't know what that means."

You turn to me again, your lips brush my cheek as you say, "It means I want you to stay here with me, Rachael. I want you to make this hotel into your dream—however you envision it. I want to give that to you."

"Why? I know you said you heard the passion for this place in my voice when we talked on the phone, but that's no reason to bring a woman you don't know down here and ask her to stay. Merrick, you don't know me."

You push up on your elbow and gaze down on me. "What do I need to know? A driven, smart, beautiful woman is in love with this hotel—just like I am. She turned it down. It's impossible to think about anyone else working on it. I swept her away like Archibald Weston with Ingrid Burkhart." You rub your thumb over my cheek. "Nobody else belongs here. I don't want to share it with anyone else. Turtle Tear's story won't be complete if you're not in it, Rachael."

God, what happened to the business savvy man I thought you were, and who replaced him with this gorgeous, romantic creature lying beside me with his eyes melting into mine.

"You know I don't have a job," I say. "I'll have to go back and find one. I can't live without money, and I can't take this on as a full time position. I've already turned it down—my mom will be coming home—" Your hand clamps down on my mouth, and you grin widely.

"I'll take care of you here. Don't worry about anything.

Your obligations will be met. Shannon will get her half of your rent. All your other bills will be paid. Everything will be taken care of." I shake my head no, but you won't take your hand off my mouth to let me refuse you. "Consider it a consulting fee if you have to."

I bite your finger and you snatch your hand away. The shocked expression on your face makes me laugh. "Weren't expecting that, were you?"

"A grown woman biting me? Well, I can't say it's never happened before, but..." You laugh and pull me up off of the hammock with you. "So will you keep the pool here?"

With my hand in yours, I follow you out into the courtyard. "I haven't said I'll do it."

You take both of my hands and stand facing me. "Let me get this straight. You don't want me to offer to take you home, so you're going to be here, but you haven't agreed to plan the renovations. So," you lean in and kiss my jaw, barely at the edge of my lips, "Rachael, why are you here?"

"Because you brought me," I say, resting my hands on your pecs and letting my head drift back as you kiss my neck.

"Why are you staying?" you whisper, tugging on my earlobe with your lips.

"Because of this." The words are out before I knew they'd been on my tongue. I don't remember thinking them. It's a completely blatant response.

"I was hoping that was the case." You pull me against

you and press your lips to mine. Your kisses are slow, savoring every second. These aren't the urgent, frantic kisses of last night. These are slow and painfully sensual.

My fingers spread on your chest feeling more of your skin. Your tongue hasn't touched mine, and I ease mine out to find yours. You pull your mouth away, grinning. "Keep it slow. We have all day."

"I thought I was in control of this?" I lift my brows at your smug expression.

"You kissed me, so kisses are fair game."

"Oh, you got the green light, so now you're taking over?" I pull away and jab my hands on my hips.

You smirk and your dimple dips in your cheek. "I apologize, ma'am. You have full authority over all physical contact between us."

"Ma'am," I mutter. "You make me sound like your grandmother."

You grab me around my hips and lift me up off my feet. "How about sex kitten? Is that better?"

I slide down your body as you slowly release me and latch onto your lips again. "Sex kitten sounds like I'm a porn star," I say between kisses.

"You kind of were last night. My own private show." You breathe out heavily into my mouth. "I've never been so turned on in my life."

"Me neither." I take your bottom lip into my mouth and tug before letting go.

"You were so hot." Your tongue traces under my upper lip.

"So were you." You lift me back up and cup my butt, urging me to wrap my legs around your waist. I smile against your lips. "What happened to taking it slow? We have all day, don't we?"

You groan and lean your forehead against mine. "You're right. And you are a sex kitten, getting me all worked up again."

"Calling me a sex kitten implies we're having sex."

"Maybe we will." You touch your nose to mine.

"Maybe we will. Maybe we won't."

"It's your call."

I nod, feeling confident and authoritative. I can bring you—a big, powerful, sexy man—to your knees right now if I wanted.

Eight

We sip iced coffee sitting on wooden stools at the rotting butcher-block island in the kitchen.

"Have them here tomorrow," you say to Joan, your assistant, on the phone. I know her name because I've been listening to half of your conversation. The first half I tried to give you privacy by lurking in the entryway while you made our coffee, but you came out and retrieved me, asking me if we should start on clearing the island and get a crew here.

"Yes, bring those too, please" you continue. Then your face lightens at what she's said and you smile, looking down into your mug. "You know me too well."

A pang of suspicion streaks through me, and I wonder about your relationship with Joan. But it's stupid of me—you and I are... I'm not sure what we are, but whatever it is, I have no reason to be jealous of anyone. I definitely hold no claim to you, nor do I want to.

You hang up and tap the phone on the counter. "Have you thought about landscaping? Should we pave trails for walking and biking around the island?"

I place my hand over your phone, silencing your tap-tap-tapping. "You do realize you sprung this on me, right? I haven't exactly thought it all through."

Narrowing your eyes, you lean forward over the counter.

"I might not know everything about you, Rachael DeSalvo, but I know you put a lot of thought into this renovation. Are you telling me you don't have *anything at all* in mind?"

I sip my coffee, lick my lips and take a deep breath readying myself to let my vision loose. "Fine. A man-made grotto on the west side with a waterfall and a swim-up bar. Private cabanas. Exotic gardens south of the cloistered courtyard with hidden niches, oversized outdoor furniture, and soft, overstuffed cushions." Your eyes shine with intensity listening to my plan. "Places to get lost in. Places to fall in love." My eyes drop from yours. You kiss your finger and place it against my lips.

"Validation," you say. "You belong here, don't you?"

I glance back up to your eyes and can't suppress my smile of agreement. "Yes."

Your face is luminous. "Do you forgive me for the way you ended up here?"

The way I got here is a dark black spot in my conscience that won't fade. I can only look into your eyes and not speak. My lips don't hold the answer you want to hear.

Your lips press tight and you lightly pound your fist onto the counter. "We'll work on it. Come on. We have trees to climb."

"Trees to climb?" I follow along behind you out the hulking, heavy hacienda door to the front of the hotel.

"Whoa," I whisper, shading my eyes with my hand. For as far as I can see, there are lines of trees weighed down with ripe fruit. Oranges, limes, mangos, figs—more fruit that I can see from where I stand. "The famed orchards of Turtle Tear."

"Where the key limes grow for the infamous key lime pie of Turtle Tear Hotel." You pick up two baskets sitting beside the front door. By the dried dirt and petals inside, I think they held flowers at one time. "Let's go pick some so I can make it for you."

"You have the recipe?" I take a basket from you, and we walk down the gentle drop of the two front stairs.

"I hope. I took a lot of cookbooks out of the kitchen and stacked them upstairs so they don't get lost. We can go through them this afternoon if you want."

"I don't have any other plans I'm aware of." I nudge you with my elbow.

"I can think of something, I'm sure." You nudge me back.

You pick up a stick and hack some of the tall grass out of our way, and we duck under the limbs of trees baring ripe, swollen fruit ready to drop onto the ground and burst open.

"I think these are key limes," you say, reaching up to pluck one off a branch. "Their rinds are lighter colored than regular limes, I believe."

"You're the Florida native," I say, holding up the basket for you. "Limes don't grow in Cleveland."

You glance down at me and frown. "I'm not a Florida native. Why did you think that?"

I scroll through my mind trying to recall when you'd

told me you lived in Florida. You never did. Why did I think you lived here? "Where are you from? Where do you live?" I really don't know you at all. I've been feeling closer and closer to you when all I've done is fill in the blanks myself.

"Georgia originally, right outside Atlanta. Heidi still lives there." You pull another lime from the branch and drop it in the basket. "I've been in upstate New York for the past five months. I move about every six months or so."

"Why so often?"

One shoulder hitches up in a shrug. "Never felt comfortable anywhere. No place felt like home I guess."

"You're considering retiring and staying here though. For how long? That's a huge decision for a six month commitment."

Holding a lime up to your nose, you take in a big sniff. "Ah." You toss it in the basket and pause, holding my gaze. "This is home, Rachael. This finally feels right."

Upstairs behind the couch in the sitting area, you lift a huge cardboard box and sit it down on the coffee table. Filled with old books, loose sheets of paper and a couple file folders, it isn't the organizational style I expected from you.

"Seriously?" I gently backhand you in the chest. "You need a filing cabinet or something. This is a mess."

You laugh, running your fingers through waves of dark hair. Your olive-toned skin has tanned a little more over the past couple days here, making your white teeth seem even whiter, your lips even redder. I'm struck by how I find every move you make sensual. Your voice vibrates through me, collects and smolders in my center.

"Organization isn't my strong suit. That's why I have Joan." You sit on the couch and hook my waistband with a finger, pulling me down next to you. "Start digging, woman. My mouth is watering thinking about that pie." Your eyebrows shrug suggestively.

"Don't get all worked up. We have all day...for pie." I pull a stack of papers and books out of the box as you chuckle, low and deep.

Instructions and a warranty for the new stove are in the first booklet I flip through. I toss it aside and grab a sheet of paper from the stack. It's faded and hand written. I can't make out one word. Beside me, you're squinting at a yellowed page in a cookbook. I pick up a file folder and leaf through.

The contents are recent. The pages have the Rocha Enterprises logo scrolled across the top. I glance to see if you're paying attention. Maybe I shouldn't be going through your business files. You're humming to yourself and running a finger down the page in the cookbook. My eyes turn back to the file on my lap.

The top page is titled: TURTLE TEAR PROJECT and it's dated 2010. I didn't realize you've owned the hotel and island that long and renovations haven't begun. Why the hold up?

The next page is a resume for a woman named Adrianna Singer. Her name is circled and beside it, in your handwriting, it says: HIRED 6/15/10. Behind Adrianna's resume is a photo of you and a dark-haired woman. You're both wearing bathing suits holding drinks served in coconuts with leis around your necks. Hawaii, maybe? Is this Adrianna? Your arm around her waist holding her close tells me she was—is?—more than an employee.

The next few pages are pink duplicates of purchase orders for building supplies, work orders for a construction crew and detailed project notes for the hotel renovation. All are dated in early 2011, and all of them have CANCELLED scratched across them in angry, black pen—in your handwriting. The last pages in the file outline a severance package for Adrianna Singer.

I slam the file shut not wanting to see anymore. You glance over, frowning. "Something wrong?"

Accusations streak through my mind, but I try to sound merely curious. "No, nothing." I hold up the file before laying it aside. "Was Adrianna Stringer hired as project manager before I was offered the job?"

Your expression freezes. Your eyes open a bit wider. "Um." You shift and cough. "She was hired with the project in mind. Negotiations on this place were still ongoing then." Your knees swivel toward me, and you lay your hand on my wrist. "Things with Adrianna...fell through."

I shake my head, reaching in the folder and pulling out the photo of you and her. "I have to ask. Do you start... *relationships* with all of your project managers, or just the brunettes?" I flick the photo, sending it spinning toward you. It hits you in the chest and falls to the floor.

You pick it up and study it. "Adrianna and I did have a relationship. It was short lived. We weren't good together. It ended badly." You toss the photo into the box on the table. "And no, I don't start relationships with all of my project managers, blonde or brunette."

"Did you…" I bite back the word kidnap and try again. "Did you *whisk* her away, too, or did she accept the job offer?"

You snatch the file off my lap, tear it in half and throw it in the box. "What do you think, Rachael? I've apologized, explained my stupid, desperate mistake and asked for your forgiveness." You throw your hands in the air. "I don't know what else to do."

You're angry, but I can't help the words that keep shooting out of my mouth. "So, did she belong here, too? Was it her dream? Was this *home* to her? Or did you just use those lines on me?"

Your hands grasp my arms and jerk me toward you. "Listen to me. Everything I've told you is the truth. I didn't use any lines on you. Adrianna wasn't right for this hotel project just like she wasn't right for me. She didn't care if she brought Turtle Tear back to life or if she was getting paid to do any other job I gave her. It was a paycheck, and I was the billionaire on her arm for a while. That's it."

"You were the billionaire on her arm for a while," I repeat. She hurt you, didn't she? It sounds like she did.

Your eyes flash, and you let go leaning back into the couch rubbing your forehead. "It doesn't matter. It's been over for a long time now."

I sit back and scoot closer to you. "In the last few days, you've told me about strained relationships between you and your dad, you and your sister, and you and this woman. Do you push people away on purpose?" I fold and rub my arms, nervous for your response.

"They push me away, Rachael, not the other way around." Your eyes are closed. My fingers twitch with the need to reach up and stroke your cheek.

"Why would they do that?" My voice is so soft; if we weren't sitting so close, you would never hear me.

You exhale loudly shaking your head. "I try. I'm always fucking things up. Look what I did to you."

My heart clenches. You're like an overeager puppy, jumping up and getting smacked back down when all you want is to be petted, cuddled, and loved.

You suck air in through your teeth rubbing your fingers through your hair vigorously. "Whatever. I'm done looking for that recipe. I'll be downstairs." You move to stand, but I grab your arm.

"Don't." I lean in and run my thumb across your cheek. "Don't run away when you should stay and talk to me."

Leaning back again, you turn and pull me against you. "Let's not talk."

Your lips meet mine, but I pull away and put my hand over your mouth. "Talk, don't kiss. It seems to me like you don't think things through before you act."

You let out a sharp laugh against my fingers, and I lower them. "I think them through. I just never come to the right conclusion. Like with you. I figured I'd get you down here and you'd be so blown away by my gesture that my impromptu, stupid plan would instantly be forgotten. I was wrong."

"How could you think that? How would you feel being drugged and taken away?"

You hold me tighter, afraid I might bolt away like the other night when our dinner turned into something way, way out of my control. "I didn't care how *I* would feel. I only thought about what you would feel if I gave all of this to you."

My shoulders sag. You don't get it. "You can't know what someone else is going to think or feel, Merrick. You have to put yourself in their position. That's the only way to judge how your words and actions are going to go over with someone else."

Your eyes look so tired, like the weight of the world rests inside you, like you've been over and over our situation and all of your failed relationships a million times and can't figure out the puzzle.

"What if I didn't want to come here?" I say, running my finger along your jaw to your ear. "What if I wanted to stay with my mom to make sure she's okay? What if I had an interview or actually cared about my internship?"

"But I took care of all of that. Your mom is happy, and she's not alone. I don't care if you had an interview because you belong here and you know it—don't tell me you don't because you already told me you do. We're going in circles, Rachael. Just let this go and forgive me. Please."

I can't resist the desperate pleading in your voice. I lean my forehead against yours. "I'm trying to forgive you."

You press me against your chest hugging me tight. "Good," you whisper in my ear. "Thank you." Your warm, soft lips find my neck and work down to my shoulder. It's intoxicating. You trail kisses down my arm and take my hand to kiss each fingertip. Fire burns behind your dark eyes. "Let's try this again," you say, pulling me down on the couch on top of you.

I sink into your lips before clearing my mind of the haze of desire and pushing myself up on your chest. "No. I'm trying, but I'm not ready for this." I get to my knees, but you hold on to my wrists and won't let me stand.

"You are ready for this. You want it as much as I do." Your chest is heaving, your eyes blazing. The pull between us is overwhelming.

"Are you going to *whisk* me into this, too? Since you know I want it. Is this something else you won't take no as an answer for?" I pull my arms free and stand, shaking, staring out the window into the bright sky.

"No." Your voice is spite, anger and pain. I close my eyes at the tone.

"I do want you. So, so bad. I can't let go though. I can't get past the barrier you shoved between us when you took all of my control away. I can't be that vulnerable again, especially not by choice. Not to you."

You shift on the couch then you're standing behind me. Your hand is in my hair, stroking and twisting down the back. "I'd never hurt you, Rachael. Never. If you gave yourself to me, it would be so good. It would be amazing."

"I know," I whisper. I can't stop shaking. I need you. I want you. I can't let myself have you.

"What can I do to fix this?" Your chest presses against my back. Your hands fall to my hips. You nuzzle your nose up and down the back of my head.

"You can't fix this."

Your hands squeeze and knead my hips. "There has to be a way."

I let my head drop back on your shoulder. Your hands feel so good. "Be patient."

"I don't have a lot of patience when it comes to this." Your lips trace my ear. Your erection presses against my lower back.

I ache for your hands to knead my breasts like they are my hips, for the back-and-forth pressure of your fingers to slide lower, between my thighs. My resolve is melting away. You cup my cheek and turn my lips to yours. My body betrays me and turns into you. My hands grasp your shoulders. My fingers glide up into the soft, waves of hair at your neck.

Your lips are hot and wet. Your tongue seeks mine and slowly brushes and caresses, drawing a moan out of me into your mouth. Your hands wrap around the back of my thighs as you lift me and sit on the couch. "Rub against me." Your hips rock into mine. "Just like before."

Your hard ridge probes between my legs, urging me

to thrust against it. I can't hold back. I'm burning. I want the mindless pleasure, the heated release. Your hands still grip my thighs and lift me up and down. I grind into you, desperate for the throbbing to be quenched. Our shirts ride up, and we're skin against skin. Our lips and tongues brush between pants of ecstasy.

I want more. I want you inside me. I want to let go.

"God, that sound you're making is driving me crazy." You tug my hair, urging my head back. Your lips devour my neck. I writhe from the mind-numbing sensation of your hot breath against my skin and dig my fingers into your bare abs. Your tongue leaves a scalding trail across my collarbone. "Come for me, Rachael."

"I need you." I whimper and moan. "I can't feel enough of you."

You groan and pull me even closer, spreading my legs wider. "Let me take you."

I gasp and clutch at your stomach. My palm presses against something round, soft and pulsing with heat. I lean my forehead against yours and glance down. Your erection has swollen out from under the waistband of your jeans, giving me an incredible view of your engorged head. I want to taste its smoothness against my lips.

I can't.

I want it.

I won't.

Your lips crush into mine. You're coming undone. Why

am I doing this to us? You could be inside me in seconds giving us both what we need.

I can't give myself over to you. This has to be on my terms, and I don't have sex without an established relationship. I barely know you, and I don't trust you.

I pull my lips away and push your shoulders back, resting my forehead against yours. "No. You have to wait until I'm ready."

Our heavy breaths come in unison. My dizzy desire ebbs, but only slightly. Your swollen tip hasn't gone back inside your pants. "Let me see you stroke yourself again."

You look up. Your dark, desperate eyes spark with intensity. "I will if you will."

I scoot down your thighs to your knees and slip my hand under my waistband. I'm crazy wet.

You pull your zipper down and ease your jeans and boxers lower, lifting your heavy balls. Your erection leans forward, long and thick. You hook my waistband with a finger. "It's no fair if I can't see you." I clamber off your lap and slip my bottoms off. You lean back, wrapping your hand around yourself. "Get back on."

I perch on your knees and you spread them wide, opening my legs. "Uh, God," you growl. "What I could do to you."

"What would you do?" I run a finger down my slit with one hand and squeeze my breast with the other. Your legs tremor underneath me.

"I'd plant my face between your thighs and make you scream my name."

I lean forward and squeeze your thigh. I'm so sensitive, if I touch my clit, I'll explode. I keep my finger running up and down, avoiding the tip to make it last. My head drops forward. You're stroking yourself right under my eyes. I lick my lips and blow on you. You gasp and jerk your hand faster, harder. I blow again.

"God, Rachael. That feels so fucking good. Let me touch you."

"No touching." I blow again, and you shudder.

You groan. "I can't take it, can't hold back. Are you ready?"

"Yes. God, yes."

You lift my chin and bore your eyes into mine. "Let go, Rachael."

With one rub of my fingertip, my body spasms and clenches. I stare into your eyes, wishing you were inside me.

You press your lips against mine, your tongue darts into my mouth as you groan and thrust one last time. I collapse against you. You hold me tight. Our chests press together, heaving to catch our breath.

"I'd rather be inside you," you say, brushing my hair out of my face, "but that was insane."

I sigh. My body trembles. You hug me and kiss my head. "I'm so relaxed."

You lay me on the couch in front of you and rest your

head on my shoulder. "If not having sex with you is this amazing, I can be patient." You glance up at me. "When will you let me touch you?"

My fingers trail through your hair. "I don't know."

"Are you punishing me?"

It's a serious question. "I don't know."

"If you are, I deserve it."

"Just be patient. I don't even know my own mind right now. You've completely turned my life upside down. I wasn't prepared for this."

"I'm sorry."

I lift your chin and search your eyes. "Merrick, do you need to be taken care of? Is that why you did it? Because you saw how I care of everybody—my mom, Shannon?"

Your eyes dart away. You can't look at me. "I've never been taken care of. I guess I don't need it."

"You want it. Don't you?"

"I take care of myself, no matter what I have to do. I find a way."

"You want it," I repeat. "Don't you?"

Your determined eyes find mine. "Yes. I want to be taken care of. And I want to take care of you. I've never felt that need before—to give what I have to someone else. To make them happy and care for them."

"And you do for me?" I can't understand how I brought this out in you.

"I feel a lot of things I've never felt before with you." Your eyes flit away, like you've revealed too much. "I can't help it. It's like I found someone who gets me. We're so alike, you and me."

I brush your cheek to bring your eyes back to mine. "How are we alike?" I need to understand what you see between us. I need to know if I see it, too.

"You're stubborn, like me. Driven, independent—when you allow yourself to be. That's not like me. I'm always independent." You laugh. "You see the potential in people, in places." You gesture to the room. "You have a firm hold on your emotions and refuse to let them stray. You give yourself," you kiss me, "on your terms."

I shake my head. He's absolutely right. "How can you know these things about me?"

You shift, rising up on your elbow to gaze down at me. "I didn't get where I am by not being able to read people. It doesn't take me long to get inside a person's head and know what's going on, what motivates them."

I nod. It's all clear now. "That's how you survived. After your mom passed and your dad neglected you. You had to take what you needed—had to know what would make people give it to you."

A crease forms between your eyes. "You make me sound like a bastard."

I smooth the crease in your forehead. "No. You did what you had to do, for you and Heidi. I think you've given more than you realize. You took care of her, didn't you?"

You lower yourself and rest your head back on my shoulder. "We took care of each other."

We stay silent, breathing slowly, relaxing in the warmth of our bodies and drift off into sleep.

When I wake, you're sitting at the end of the couch sorting through the papers in the box on the coffee table. My calves rest on your leg. I'm still naked from the waist down, and your shirt is off. I'm guessing it was a little messy.

A golden-hued light streams in through the window. It shines behind you, gilding your profile. I sit up and stretch. It must be late afternoon. You smile and rub a hand over my head, ruffling my messy hair. "You must've been worn out."

"Guess I was." Emotionally worn out. Physically, I had a long way to go to reach worn. I slide my bottoms back on. "Still looking for that recipe?"

"I thought it was here, but I guess it's not." You toss a stack of index cards and a notebook back into the box. "I'm glad you're up. Perfect timing." You stand and pull me to my feet.

"Perfect timing for what?"

"Sunset."

"How long did I sleep?" I feel like I'm lost in some kind of time warp.

"You slept all afternoon. So did I." Your thumb rubs across the back of my hand. "I haven't slept so well in a long, long time." You slowly lean forward and kiss me. It's tender, intimate. It lingers. When our lips part, I take a deep breath, reeling. Do I want intimacy with you? I can't even accept a purely physical relationship. But I always demand the intimacy first. Nothing is only physical with me.

"I'm going to pack us a picnic." You kiss me again, quickly this time and dash out of the room.

I collapse back onto the couch and attempt to get my head together. Are you insane, or just badly misunderstood? Am I insane for wanting to be with you? One minute I'm ready to dive in with you, and the next I'm standing hesitant on the shore questioning everything.

Ugh, I'm making myself crazy.

I rub the heels of my hands over my eyes, and my cell phone rings. I jolt to the edge of the couch. My heart beats wildly. My wristlet, with my phone tucked inside, sits on the coffee table beside the box.

It rings again.

Do I answer it? What do I say?

A third ring.

I can't get my hands to move. What if they ask questions? When did I decide to come down here? I'm not a spur-of-the-moment kind of girl. How do I explain it? Do I tell the truth?

Fourth ring.

Shit. What do I do? My fingers clutch the collar of my t-shirt—your t-shirt. My eyes stare a hole through my wristlet.

No more ringing. The call must've gone to voicemail.

I hunch back into the couch, trying not to question why I didn't answer it. I don't need anything more to analyze.

Nine

"This is amazing." My voice echoes in my ears through my headset. "You can see the whole island from up here." I grip my seat with sweaty hands as you fly us high over the island in your helicopter. My stomach drops and lurches each time we turn or dip, but my fear of heights has gone right out the window with the stunning view. The sunset is a spectacular sight when you're right in the midst of it. Orange, pink, and gold streaks stripe the blinding blue sky as it fades to gray.

You stare at me with a smile on your face and the oddest expression in your eyes. It's almost like reverence. "What?" I ask. "Why are you looking at me like that?"

"Your reaction makes every year I worked my ass off to be able to own luxuries like this helicopter worth it." I didn't think your voice could affect me more, but through the mic it reverberates low and deep in my headphones.

I turn away, pretending to be enraptured with the view more than the look in your eyes. I could get lost in them if I let myself. It's unsettling. You make an amused sound, like you want to laugh. You know you're getting under my skin. It's obvious I'm holding onto my resolve by a thread. A fine, fraying thread.

You fly us around the island, stopping to hover by the

boathouse. "Look." You say in your headset, pointing to the bank where we shoved off into the water in the fishing boat. "See him? I told you there were gators around here."

Scooting to the edge of my seat, I lean over you to see and rest my hand on your thigh. You lower your hand on top of mine. "I don't see it." I squint, but can't make out any movement or alligator shapes on the shore.

"He's in the water now, about to go under."

I give you a sideways glance, and you start laughing. "You made it up."

Your arm circles my waist, and you tug me closer to you. "I'll admit it. It was a ploy to get you to slide over here."

"Sneaky."

"Strategic."

"Is it always about winning with you?"

A sly grin hitches across your lips. "No. It's mostly about sex." You pat the picnic basket behind us. "And food. It's mostly about food and sex."

My chest and neck flush, and I grin back at you. "Is that why you brought a blanket?"

Your eyebrows shoot up. "Well no, but I like where you're going with this."

Oh, God. My mind's in the gutter. Why do you do this to me?

Your smile grows wide, dimples showing. "Your face is blood red. Why are you embarrassed? It's not like we haven't shared a moment...or two."

"I know. I was there." Taking a deep breath to calm

myself, I glance out the side of the helicopter again. I feel like I'm sitting on top of the sun—too close, too hot.

Your fingers stroke up and down my side. "I'll put us down. I have a special place to show you."

"This entire island is a special place."

"This is more special. And secret. I was thinking you might want to keep it that way—secret—just for the two of us."

"What is this special place?"

Curiosity makes me turn back to look at you. My breath stutters. You can't keep the wide smile off your face. Your brown eyes glow amber in the setting sunlight. Waves of dark hair blow across your forehead. You exude sexuality. I know it's helpless. I'll give in the next time you kiss me. I'm not strong enough to resist.

"You'll find out soon enough." Your hand runs up through my hair, and you squeeze the back of my neck. "Dinner comes with a free massage. Lucky you."

"You're trying to get around the no touching rule."

"I'm touching you right now."

I lean my head back as you squeeze. "Not where it counts."

"Hmm...tell me where it counts."

"You know where it counts." God, your fingers feel good.

"I want to hear you say it. What do you call it, Rachael?"

"What do *you* call it, Merrick?"

You chuckle. "Right now I'm calling it The Forbidden Destination and trying like hell to find a map."

I press my lips together suppressing a laugh. "Keep trying, you're getting closer."

You shift in your seat. "You're making me hard again."

"Oh, I could take care of that for you, too." Your eyes meet mine. "If you had that map."

A deep groan growls from your throat, and you squeeze my neck again. "You're going to keep me at arm's length forever. I'm going to die on this island with the bluest set of balls ever found on a man."

"Don't you have an assistant for that, too?"

Your hand flinches then freezes on the back of my neck, but you don't respond.

We start descending back toward the grassy area where you keep the helicopter. I've struck a nerve, but I'm not sure why. Are you sleeping with Joan? Were you at one time? Something happened to make you react this way. "I'm sorry if I said something I shouldn't have."

Your fingers work into my neck again. "You didn't."

But I did. I crossed a line. The thought of Joan arriving tomorrow makes my stomach clench. It's odd how quickly I've gone from wanting off this island to wanting to stay here *alone* with you for a while longer. I don't want Joan interfering before I get sure footing with you.

The copter bumps down onto the ground. You flip some switches and pull your headset off. I do the same. "Don't move," you tell me.

I wait until you come around to my side and help me down. You take the picnic basket in one hand and place the other on top of my head to make sure I bend down with you, clearing the propeller slowly rotating to a stop. "It's not far from here," you say.

Unlike the first time you showed me the helicopter, we don't head through the Mangroves toward the water. This time, we walk the opposite direction through the grass and into the trees. They're just as dense, but don't have the cage-like root systems that make it almost impossible to get through. These trees are tall and fat, solid with high, leafy branches. Moss trails down like streamers blowing in the breeze. You approach one and hold the basket out to me. "I'll lower a hook down for the basket."

I'm confused until you start climbing a ladder—or rather, wooden planks nailed to the tree trunk. Following the boards up the tree, my eyes land on the underside of a massive tree house. "Oh, wow. How did you find this?"

"I got lost on my way from the helicopter to the hotel the first time I came here. Wandered around for a few hours then leaned against this tree. One of the nails ripped a hole in my shirt."

"Is it safe?" I grab a board try to wiggle it. It doesn't budge.

"As far as I can tell." You take a few more steps up and disappear through the square hole in the floor. A few seconds later, you appear leaning over the side of a railing. "Okay, hook the basket on to this, and I'll haul it up. Can you make it up the ladder? I can come down and get you."

"I can climb a ladder, Merrick. You're the old man here. I'm only twenty-five."

I can't see you anymore, but I hear you laugh. As I reach up to grab hold of a board, you yell, "Watch out for snakes."

I jerk my hand back to my chest. "Very funny. Now you might have to come down and get me."

"How about I lower the hook? You can stick it in your pants and I'll pull you up. I'd like to see you with a massive wedgie."

"And somehow you've reverted to the humor of a fifth grader." I start climbing, grinning hugely.

"I'm saving my fart jokes for later."

"You're *sure* you're Merrick Rocha, the billionaire real estate god? I'm starting to think you're an impersonator." I reach the top and grab the floor through the opening. Your hands grasp my wrists, and you pull me up to my knees. You're kneeling, and we're face-to-face.

"I'm just Merrick, okay? Nothing else. Just a regular guy."

I nod, but you'll never be just a regular guy. Regular guys don't buy islands with historic hotels on them. Regular guys don't own helicopters and have their assistants fly in food to stock their kitchen. Regular guys don't *whisk* women away—if that's what we're calling it.

We settle onto the red and green plaid blanket, and you open the basket. "Water, pasta salad, olives." You pull each item out one at a time, taking lids off of plastic containers and setting them in the center between us. "Grilled rose-mary chicken and chocolate, raspberry cake for dessert."

I pop a green olive in my mouth. "When did you put all of this together?"

"I cooked a lot when we first got here." You frown, busying your hands with napkins and silverware. "You slept for quite a while." Your eyes find mine. "You slept so long, I was afraid I'd hurt you."

A wave of anger rolls through me. "You said you'd never done that before—put something in a woman's drink. How did you get it? How did you know how to use it?"

"A guy in the men's room offered it to me for twenty bucks. I didn't even think about it. I paid him, found you and bought you a drink. It seemed like the answer I'd been waiting for."

I grit my teeth. *"It wasn't an answer."*

"I know that. It was stupid. Dangerous. I could've hurt you. If I'd given you too much…" Your hand flies to your head. Your fingers pull at your hair. "I was seconds from taking you to a hospital when you finally woke up."

I pull my knees up and wrap my arms around them. "I don't believe you. How would you have explained what happened to me? You would've been arrested."

Your eyes glaze over, glaring at me. "You think I'd let you die?"

I flinch. "I—"

"I gave you your phone. You can call 911 any time. I offered to take you home. Why would I do that if I was afraid of being arrested?" You jam a bottle of water back into the picnic basket. Plates rattle and clank. "I wouldn't let you fucking die." You voice is quiet, steel.

On your feet, you lean your elbows on the railing. Both hands run over your head, fingers gripping and sliding through your hair in frustration. "If I could go back to that night, I'd leave you alone and find a way to forget you. Nobody has ever distrusted me like you do. It's eating away at me. I can't fix it. I can't make you forget. You'll always think of me as the monster who abducted you."

I swallow hard against the sob gathering in my throat. "You're not a monster."

You let out an indignant snort and pound your fists against the railing. "I'll take you home."

Your words are a slap to my conscience. Panic digs its fingernails into my spine. I'm on my feet and standing behind you in an instant. "No."

You turn to me, your face a cocktail of guilt, surprise and reluctance. "I'll take you home, Rachael. You don't want to stay here with me."

"My mom called," I say, grasping at anything I can think to convince you. "I didn't answer it. I didn't know what to tell her. I didn't want to be tempted to tell the truth," I glance down at my feet, "and leave you."

You push away from the railing, squat down and start packing food back into the picnic basket. "Call her back. Tell her your consulting job is finished, and you'll be home in the morning."

I dive to my knees beside you, pulling your hands out of the basket so I can take them in mine. But you nudge me away from you. "I wanted you Rachael, and not as an employee." You grab the olives, sending them rolling over the blanket and deck. "You're right, I don't think. I act. I do whatever I need to, to get what I want. I fuck everything up—all the time. We were fucked before we had a chance to even begin." You reach in the basket, come out with a handful of chocolate cake and throw it against the side of the tree house. "Fuck."

You sit and lean against the railing with your knees up and your forearms propped on top of them. Your fingers dangle, your right hand covered in chocolate. With your head hanging, chin to chest, I can't see your eyes.

Doubt and uncertainty circle through my chest. I should let you take me home, but I don't want to. I can't stop my insane infatuation with you—a tortured, misunderstood, miserable man I can't get enough of. I'm walking straight into the lion's den, and I don't even care. I only run faster.

You sigh and glance up at me. I can't stand the anguish in your eyes. I crawl to you and sit on my knees at your feet. Your expression is filled with unasked questions. In answer, I take your wrist and lift your chocolate-covered hand to my mouth. Very slowly, I run my tongue from the bottom of your palm to the tip of your middle finger. You close your eyes and exhale deeply.

With my free hand, I push against your knee, sliding your legs apart and scooting in between them. Closer to you now, I put your index finger in my mouth and caress it with my tongue. Dark chocolate and raspberry make my mouth water. I suck your finger and slowly pull it out of my mouth.

You watch me glide the tip of your ring finger over my lips leaving a smear of frosting that my tongue eagerly licks away. "Why are you doing this to me?" you whisper. "You don't want me."

I can't answer you in words. All I know is what my body is telling me. I suck your pinkie and lick it clean. With only your thumb left, I bring it to my neck and trail a line of chocolate down to my chest. I lift myself higher on my knees and tilt my head, my eyes daring you to resist me.

Your chest heaves. The muscles in your arms clench. You want this. "I want this," I whisper, and that's all it takes to ignite you.

You press me against your chest with your hands splayed across my back, your open mouth sliding up my throat. You groan into the soft indentation at the base of my neck, sending thrilling vibrations through my body. I gasp and pull you even closer. I'm breathing so hard; I can't catch my breath. Your hands tangle in my hair and tug my head further back. Your tongue scorches a trail up my neck to my chin. Then your lips capture mine. We're panting into each other's mouths. Tongues tangling, pushing, stroking. Nothing has ever felt as good as you.

"Don't take me back," I beg. "I never thought I'd be here."

Your hands climb to my neck; your mouth moves to my

chin, my cheeks, back to my mouth. "Never. I'll never take you back."

We lean our foreheads together, sticky and sweaty, dizzy and drunk on one another, your hands on my face, mine in your hair. "Help me get past this."

"I'm trying."

I stroke your cheek. "Don't give up on me."

You chuckle. "I'm supposed to say that." Your fingers gently pull strands of hair away from my neck where it's stuck to my skin. "If I had it to do over, I'd go right to your door and talk to you. I'd take my time, ask you out for coffee, convince you to come down here with me—just for a weekend—long enough to let this place sink into you. You'd choose to be here and never leave. Then we wouldn't have this...situation standing in our way."

I rub my cheek over yours, delighting in the sensation of soft stubble prickling my skin. "I know you didn't mean me harm," I whisper in your ear.

Your lips slide along my jaw to my ear. "I won't hurt you. You can trust me, Rachael."

"Be patient." I spread my hands across your broad, strong chest and lay my head on your shoulder.

Your hand cups my cheek. "I'll wait forever for you if I have to."

We sit in the last remaining moments before darkness falls, perfectly still until our breathing steadies and our hearts stop pounding. "I'm sorry I spilled the olives," you say. "You were eating those."

"Somehow most of our meals together end up forgotten." I brush my lips lightly over yours. "I'm okay with it though."

"I'll get everything back out." Your finger runs up and down my arm. "But I don't want to move right now."

I nuzzle my nose in close under your ear. "Don't move. Stay right here."

When the first few stars blink in the sky, I take your hand and lead you back onto the blanket. We lay side by side, our folded hands resting over your heart, letting ourselves be smothered by the darkness.

The rapid, steady beat of helicopter blades wakes me the next morning. I dart up onto my knees and press my face against the window pane, trying to see it flying overhead. I can't spot it in the blinding white sun, but know where it's headed.

You're not in the room. We came back late. Both of us had fallen asleep in the tree house. After tucking me into bed and placing a chaste kiss on my lips, you retreated to the couch to sleep. I check the time on my phone. Seven-thirty. I wonder what woke you so early.

I quickly shower, scrubbing off sticky chocolate residue, dress, and head downstairs.

Voices greet me on my way through the lounge. Yours and someone else's—a woman's. The two of you sit at the wrought iron table on the patio sipping coffee.

She's in my seat.

You see me and jump up. "Morning." You're all smiles, rushing toward me. "Rachael, this is Joan, my assistant."

The leggy blonde stands and holds out her hand. "Nice to meet you, Rachael. I brought you a wardrobe so you don't have to wear Merrick's clothes anymore."

I wonder if all of your employees call you by your first name. "Thank you." I shake her hand and glance down at myself wearing your t-shirt and baggy basketball shorts cinched tight at the waist. I like wearing them.

You pull out the chair on the other side of yours, across the round table from Joan. "I'll get your coffee." You plant a kiss on top of my head and disappear inside.

Joan raises an eyebrow and gives me a smug smile. "Well. I've never seen him like this. He's the one who gets waited on hand and foot, certainly not the other way around."

"He's been very attentive," I mutter, wishing she didn't look quite so perfect in her short red sundress and spiky heels. "Did you come alone?"

"Yes, I was dropped off first thing this morning to coordinate the arrival of the work crew and building supplies." Her red fingernails tap against her mug. "And to touch base with Merrick privately before things got crazy around here." She laughs, but it's fake.

I tap my teeth together. I don't like the sound of this woman having private time with you. My intuition tells me her motivation isn't work related at all.

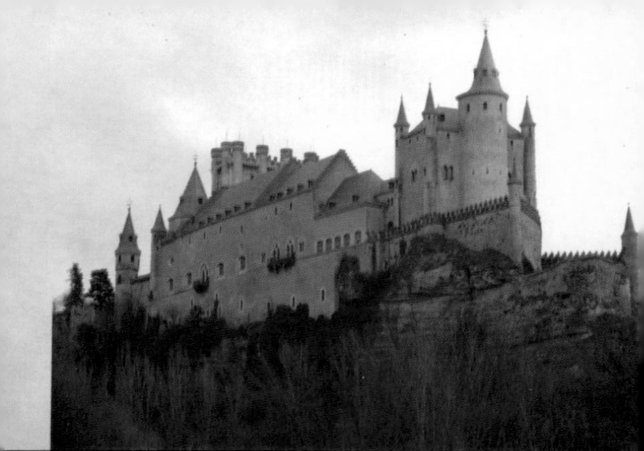

PATRONATO DEL ALCAZAR DE SEGOVI

después de la hora de cierre.
Se deberá abandonar el Alcázar, como máximo, 30 minutos
dad. Conserve esta entrada hasta el final de la visita.
promiso de observar las normas de funcionamiento y seguri-
ción y uso de esta entrada conlleva la aceptación y el com-
El importe de esta entrada no es reembolsable. La introduc-

SOLO PALACIO
06-04-2009
18:24:36
Precio. 4,00 Euros

C.I.F. Q-4078001-G
www.alcazardesegovia.com
PATRONATO DEL ALCAZAR DE SEGOVIA

I shouldn't be jealous. I barely know you, and Joan obviously does—well.

You stride back out through the patio doors and set a mug of coffee and dish of fruit in front of me. "You have to be starving. Joan and I are wrapping up here then I'll make us breakfast." You squeeze my shoulder. "Wow, you're tense." You stand behind me and massage my shoulders for a few minutes while Joan sips her coffee with her back ramrod straight and keeps her eyes glued to her mug.

"When will the crew arrive?" I ask, leading the conversation back to business.

Joan picks up her phone and taps a few times on the screen. "Forty-three minutes from now." She opens a file folder and directs her question to you. "Will they start on the hotel or the pool and cabana area today?"

You sit and look at me, smiling. "Rachael?"

Joan's eyes widen and shift to me. She doesn't say a word.

"You and I can begin clearing out some of the guest rooms," I say to you, ignoring Joan. "The crew will need somewhere to sleep. They can start on the pool area and work their way to the hotel once we've got everything we'd like to use in the restoration safely stored away somewhere."

You knock your knuckles on the tabletop. "Perfect. Got that Joan?"

"Oh, I've got it." She makes a few notes in her file before she stands. "I need to get to the landing area. Enjoy your morning." She shoves a pair of sunglasses on her face and strides out through the gate.

"I have no idea how she's going to make her way around the island in those heels," I say, watching her go.

"She's very resourceful," you say, following her every stride.

"I figured." I pop a grape in my mouth and crush it between my teeth.

You give me an uncertain look, like you're not sure at all what I'm thinking. "Are you okay?"

"Fine." I force a smile onto my lips. "Thanks for the coffee and fruit."

"You're welcome." Leaning back in your chair, your lips curve slightly at the corners and your eyes trail over my face. "I love how your skin glows in the morning sunlight. It's been one of my favorite parts of having you here with me."

My chest surges with nervous excitement. I can't pull my eyes away from you. You're so at peace. I've never seen you without a hint of torment playing over your face. Your fingers come up and teepee under your chin. Suddenly, the peaceful look is gone, and your brows furrow. "I never even considered…"

"What?"

"Do you have someone? A boyfriend? Someone I took you away from?"

"Did you see me with someone while you were watching me?"

A shadow crosses your face and then it's gone. "No repeat offenders."

I secretly enjoy the fact that you saw me going out with other men, and it bothered you. "If I did have someone, I suppose the relationship would be over now, don't you think? My leaving without saying a word about it would put a strain on things."

One eyebrow cocks up. "But you didn't?"

I shake my head. "No. I didn't."

Your hands fall, and you grasp the arms of the chair, exhaling noisily. "Thank God. I didn't need one more hurdle between us to leap."

"That's what I'm talking about though," I say, leaning forward. "You need to take the feelings of others into consideration."

You reach for my hand and place yours over it on the table. "I'm trying. It's been about me for so long. I've grown accustomed to being selfish." You lace your fingers with mine. "I promise you, anything I do from here on out will be to make you happy."

Despite the fact that you're getting ahead of yourself—and me—your words fill me with warmth. "If you can do that for me, you can do it for Heidi."

Your hand squeezes mine. "When this restoration is well under way and the hotel is fit for guests, I'll bring her and my brother-in-law and niece and nephew down to see it. And to meet you, if I haven't run you off."

"Let's take us day-by-day. I think your sister and her

family would love it here. Maybe we should put a slide in the pool."

"The kids would love that." Your smile is enormous, infectious.

"Merrick, you know that one kind gesture might not fix everything between the two of you, right?"

Your smile falters a little. "I know. But it'll be a good start."

"A very good start." I push a strawberry around in my bowl, thinking about how to ask you what I'm wondering and deciding the best approach is to just ask. "Does Heidi talk to your father? How does she feel about the lawsuit?"

Your fingers slide from between mine as you sit back in your chair. "She talks to him. She wasn't very active in the company when he started demanding money, so it didn't affect her like it has me."

"Does it bother you that she talks to him?"

You sit forward again and lean your elbows on your knees, careful to not make eye contact with me. "I don't want her to pick sides. It's best if she stays out of it."

"But does it *bother you*, Merrick?"

You sigh and furiously rub the back of your head. "I was the one who took care of her—the one who has always taken care of her. Even after she got married, I..."

"You what? Took care of her better than her husband?"

"Yes. Don't get me wrong, the guy loves her. I know that. But she's got herself a younger version of my father. He doesn't show her a lot of affection, and I hate to see her begging for it. God, it's like some kind of mind-fuck just watching her wrestle with herself over holding his hand or touching his arm. Can't he just reach out and take her hand? Would it kill him to show her he loves her?"

You lean back and bring your hands down, squeezing your knees. Pain sears your eyes. "Can't someone be on my side for once? Someone I don't sign a paycheck for? Am I that bad?"

My heart clenches. Words pool on my tongue. *I'll be on your side.* But how can I say them? How can I think them? Are you that bad? I don't know what you're capable of, where your limits lay.

I can't take seeing you like this. "I'll make breakfast," I say, standing and collecting my coffee mug and fruit dish.

"No." You shift to your feet and try to take the bowl from me. "I was planning on it. It's no problem. I want to."

"Let me. Please." I need to do something for you. I can't promise to be on your side. Not yet. But, I need to give you something—make a gesture to ease you.

A helicopter flies over, followed by another. "Sounds like you're going to be needed outside of the kitchen," I say, pulling the fruit dish back from your fingers. "You might trust Joan with all of the details, but I just met her. I'd be more comfortable knowing you were there to oversee things. I'll be here making breakfast." You won't refuse a request if it's about the renovations. You put me in charge after all.

A smile slips across your lips and you narrow your dark, brooding eyes. "That's a very sneaky tactic, Miss DeSalvo."

"It's called strategy, Mr. Rocha."

Your laugh shakes any remaining anguish from your expression. "You are the boss. I'll go and make sure everything is on schedule, but I won't be gone long. Don't get comfortable being without me."

As you take the path through the gate, I step inside the hotel, and I puzzle at your last words. *Don't get comfortable being without me.* Are you afraid to leave me alone? Afraid my thoughts of how crazy this situation is will get the better of me? If you hadn't infiltrated my every waking hour, there's a good chance I would've taken you up on your offer to take me back home.

You've muscled your way in. I feel the separation now that I'm here by myself, footsteps echoing down this hallway into an empty kitchen. I'm anxious for you to come back and fill the space with—you. With your smile and energy, your voice and laughter.

God, help me. I'm falling for you. How did I allow you under my skin like this? How can I get you out? A niggling in my brain goes off like a small alarm. I don't want to get you out of my system.

I like you in here.

Ten

More than an hour has passed and I've got enough eggs and bacon staying warm in the oven for all of the crew and Joan—if she even eats. Given her size, it's debatable.

There's no broom in the hotel that I can find, so I've broken down a cardboard box and use it to sweep the shards of glass on the entryway floor into a pile in the corner. Two large suitcases sit right inside the kitchen that I ignore, certain my new wardrobe is folded neatly inside them. I'm not eager to accept it. Then again, it isn't like accepting charity—you brought me here with no clothes.

What type of clothing would Joan pick out for me? I can only imagine. I'm going to be renovating an historic hotel in stilettos and spaghetti straps with a thong riding up my ass. If that's the case, I'm sticking to wearing your clothes.

"Hey," you say, strolling in behind me, "what are you doing? I'll get that. The crew brought a broom and all the tools we'll need to start working around this place." You're bare from the waist up, damp and glistening from the sun and practically glowing. "I rescued something just in time." You step back and peer down the hall toward the lounge, then beckon someone with your hand.

Two men lumber into the entryway hauling a long

wooden beam. I spy the etched heart with two sets of initials inside and recognize it immediately. "Thank God you remembered!" I rush forward and run my fingertips over the heart. "This can never get lost."

Your smile is enormous, and you rock up on your toes with your hands shoved into the pockets of your faded jeans that fit every sculpted muscle. "I get the important things right, Rachael."

Not sure how to respond, I only blink a few times before turning to the men holding the beam. "Please, lean it against the wall and come have some breakfast. I've made enough for everyone," I say, turning to Merrick. "Will you go get them?"

You rub the back of your neck. "I'm sure they ate before they arrived. We should really get them going on the cabana."

"Let's call it a kick-off meeting then to get everyone on the same page. Please go get them." I'm not wasting the food I made and the time I put into preparing it. I'm trying to do something nice, don't you realize?

You're hesitant. "Can I talk to you for a minute?" You nod toward the stairs.

Why do you have to over think this? "What?"

You nod again, and I follow you halfway up the steps. Stopping, you take my hand. Your face is focused, eyes dark and gleaming with power. "Don't blur the line between employer and friend with these guys."

"Like you and Joan?" The words tumble out, and I want to scoop them up and shove them back in, but I can't.

You jerk back, shocked and quirk an eyebrow. Are you amused? "I mean it. They'll take advantage of the situation if they can and screw off. You have to stay on top of them." Your lips twist. "Not literally though, please. I'll end up as jealous of the crew as you seem to be of Joan." A sly, sexy grin forms on your lips.

"Why would I ever be jealous of Joan?" I spin on my heel, but before I can take one step down the stairs, you've got me by the shoulders.

"You shouldn't ever be jealous of Joan," you say, your mouth close to my ear, your warm breath tickling my neck. "You're all I want."

I shouldn't ask. It's none of my business, but I have to know. "Have you been with her?"

You squeeze my shoulders, and I'm so tense, it hurts. "Physically, yes. Emotionally, no."

My eyes squeeze shut. "Recently?"

"Define recent." Your fingers tighten on my shoulders again. Your thumbs dig into my back and massage.

"I don't think I need to. You've just answered my question." I push your hands off of me and stride down the stairs. The woman you're involved with knows every detail of your life—plans every detail of your life. Now she's here. How nice for you.

I storm into the kitchen and fling the oven door open. Grabbing a pot holder, I yank the baking sheets and casserole dishes out and slam them onto the marble island. *Fucking asshole*. Why would you bring me here if you're

with her? Why would you make me start to have feelings…?
Fucking asshole!

"Guys," I hear you say out in the entryway, "go get the rest of the crew and tell them Miss DeSalvo has called a breakfast meeting."

Work boots clomp away, and even if I don't hear you come in, I can feel your presence in the kitchen with me. "Rachael, what do you want me to say? I didn't expect you to react this way."

"I'm not reacting any way. Just getting things ready for the meeting." If you come near me right now, I'll kill you. I can't even look at you or I'll throw something at your head.

You take two hesitant steps toward me. "This isn't reacting?"

My eyes dart to yours. I feel mine blazing as if they could shoot lasers. "You'll know when I'm reacting, Merrick. Trust me." My finger slips off of the potholder and scorches onto a glass casserole dish. "Ow!"

You dart forward and grab my hand. "Under cold water. Now."

I yank my hand away. "Don't tell me what to do!"

Your fingers clamp over my wrist. Now your eyes could shoot lasers. "Stop." You wrap your other arm around my waist and lead me to the sink. "You're so damn stubborn."

"You're—" I clench my teeth. "A lot of things."

A bark of laughter shoots out of you. "A lot of bad things?"

"Mostly."

You hold my hand under ice cold water and rest your chin on my shoulder. "Not all bad things I hope."

"Right now, I'm struggling to think of something good."

"It was only sex. She means nothing to me. I haven't been with her since the day I interviewed you on the phone. I haven't wanted anyone else since then."

I huff. "I don't believe that."

You spin me around and lower your head so we're eye-to-eye, our noses almost touching. "Believe it."

I breathe you in. My eyelids fall to half-mast, heavy with desire. "Prove it," I whisper.

The tip of your nose caresses mine. "How?"

"Find a way."

The noisy conversation of a group of men and boots clomping toward the kitchen makes us straighten and step apart. I catch my breath, watching your eyes go from blazing hot with arousal to a more natural warm. "Your men have arrived, Miss DeSalvo."

"My men," I mutter, my mind rattled. "Right."

You smile and your eyes crinkle at the corners. "Need a minute to collect yourself? I can get this started."

"I hate you."

"No you don't." Your lips brush mine.

"I want to."

"I know." Your stroke my cheek with the back of your hand. "I'm glad you don't though."

A feminine, "Ehem," breaks our contact. "Are we interrupting?" Joan wears a toxic, irritated expression. "We were told you wanted to meet with us, Rachael." She says my name like it's poison rolling off her red lips.

"Yes." Taking her in, a tremor runs though me. She's been with you.

Your hand presses against the small of my back. "Have a seat everyone," you say. "There are some chairs—feel free to sit on the counters. I'm afraid we don't have enough seating for everyone."

"This will need to be fast." Joan flips through her planner. "We don't have time to indulge in unscheduled breakfast meetings."

"We have time to indulge in whatever Miss DeSalvo wishes us to indulge in." Your voice is full of threat. She's treading the line. She sniffs and tilts her chin in the air, but doesn't respond.

I open the cupboard and haul out an armful of plates. "Go ahead and get some food. I want to thank you all for coming on such short notice." Joan's eyes pop to the size of silver dollars like treating the work crew like human beings is simply not heard of. "There's a lot to do around here. When it's finished, I hope you will all come back with your loved ones and enjoy it." I glance at you out of the corner of my eye. "On the company, of course, as a way of saying thank you."

The men start commenting to each other about how awesome a free vacation will be and thanking me as they fill their plates.

Beside me, you stiffen and raise a hand. "Given we meet our deadline for renovations. It won't be easy."

"I'm sure we'll make it," I say, cutting you off. You want me in charge; you've got me in charge. "I'm sure Joan has shown you the plans for the pool area and cabana. Once that's complete, you'll start on the hotel."

"They've seen the blueprints, Rachael," Joan says, speaking to me like I'm a child. "They know what to do."

"Good. What will you be doing then?" I tilt my head and raise my eyebrows. "Are you their supervisor, or is there one on the crew? A foreman maybe?"

You cough beside me then turn to the sink and grab a glass for water. I think you might be choking on my words. The clink of silverware and dull mumble of the men stops.

"Overseeing the process," she says, her words as cold and smooth as steel.

"When you're not *overseeing the process*?" I say, narrowing my eyes. She will know where she stands with me. "You can help me cook, clean and take the helicopter to the nearest grocery store. I'm sure the men will need a lot of food to keep their energy up."

Her eyes are calling me a bitch, but her mouth says, "Fine."

You down a glass of water, but stay turned around, leaned against the sink. Your shoulders shake like you're laughing. She watches you, and her face flames.

Just like that, I feel terrible for her. Did she know it

was only sex? Even if she did, I can tell she wanted more. "Thank you for organizing everything, Joan. I appreciate it."

"It's my job," she says curtly.

"Not cooking and cleaning, so thank you."

You've turned around, and you're looking at me like I've grown a second head in the last thirty seconds. If *your* second head hadn't led her on, maybe I could be a bitch to her without feeling guilty. I glare at you for a moment before grabbing a plate. "There's plenty of food, so help yourselves to more. I'm looking forward to getting to know all of you."

Beside me again at the island, you pick up a fork and tap it in your palm. "Nicely handled."

"Nothing was handled. It was just a gesture on my part. I want them to like me."

Your forehead creases. "They don't have to like you. They have to do what you say, or they don't get paid."

"They'll do more for me if they like me." I grab your fork to stop your fiddling with it. "You've heard the expression: You catch more bees with honey than vinegar, haven't you?"

"I'm not a beekeeper. I'm a CEO." You snatch your fork back.

"You're—a lot of things."

Your lips twist and you grab a piece of bacon and point it at me. "Honey. I'll keep that in mind."

I lean forward and bite the end of your bacon. "You do that."

You shake your head slightly and lean in to my ear. "These jeans aren't discrete enough for you to do this to me."

"Mmm..." I chew and take another bite from the bacon between your fingers.

"You're making a spectacle of us."

A man approaches us. His blonde hair is pulled back in a ponytail, and the black lines of a tattoo sneak from under the arm of his t-shirt down his bicep. He's built—and hot. I blink a few times. You take my hand and squeeze, reminding me who brought me here. Jealous?

"Miss DeSalvo, I'm Beck Tanner, crew foreman. What you're planning to do here is amazing. We're all glad to be a part of it." His eyes are bright, and it's like there's a live current running through them. He has so much energy streaming through his veins.

You squeeze my hand again. Feeling threatened? "Thank you," I say. "It's a vigorous schedule. Do you foresee any issues?"

"We've discussed the schedule at length," Joan says, coming forward with a click-clack of her heels. "It will be tight. There might be some issues—"

"With the motivation of a free vacation," Beck says, cutting her off with a brilliant smile, "there won't be issues. My guys will work around the clock if they have to. It's a very generous gift. Thank you."

"Very generous," Merrick repeats, stuffing the rest of his bacon into his mouth.

"You're welcome. Everyone needs incentives." I lift a baking sheet to Beck. "Toast?"

He takes a piece and tears a bite off, winking at me. "Delicious breakfast, too. I might move into the hotel after the job's done."

You inhale a deep breath. "I need to check on something. Do you need me here any longer?"

I shake my head. "No. I've got it covered."

"More than covered," you mumble behind me as you leave.

Joan swivels and follows you out, making my stomach clench. She's like your shadow, and what's the deal with the Mr. Moody routine all of a sudden? Like it's my fault Beck's a flirt.

"Everything okay?" he asks, watching you and Joan stalk off.

"Just fine." I give him my most convincing smile, but don't think he's convinced.

"If you say so. Let me know if you need anything. I'll find you later tonight to give you the daily report."

"Daily report?"

"Just a quick update on our progress. I know Dragon Lady tracks the progress of the projects, but I'd much rather deal with you." He winks again and turns back to his men.

Dragon Lady. Ha! I want to laugh, but it wouldn't be professional. I probably should've stuck up for her and asked him not to call her that again. Probably—but didn't— oh well.

Not finding you anywhere in the hotel, I wander outside. My hands are pruney from washing a million dishes, and my finger has a blister on it where it's burned.

I follow the path to the pool. The tall grass and vines along the trail have been cut back with a weed whacker. I still hear it humming in the distance. I guess it would be easier to carry equipment and supplies through here without being tripped up by Mother Nature.

The crew comes into view, tearing down the roof of the covered cloister where you and I swung in the hammock. I wonder what you did with the rope hammock. I hope you saved it.

A radio blares, hammers pound, saws buzz. Shirtless men in cut-off shorts toss scraps of wood into a pile and take measurements. Joan sits cross-legged in a lawn chair in the shade talking on her cell phone, but you're nowhere in sight.

"Hey! Miss DeSalvo!" Beck calls from up on a ladder. He nods his head farther down the trail. "I believe you'll find what you're looking for by the water." He shoots me his trademark wink.

"Thanks!" I square my shoulders and walk past Joan, who doesn't bother looking up at me.

It's sweltering under the direct sun beating down on my head and shoulders. Bees drift lazily over wildflowers, and I think about my comment to you—how you'll try to remember to be more honey-like.

You're very honey-like around me. I understand your reluctance to let your charming side show in business relationships, but you honestly have no idea how to deal with people in your personal life. Honey would help all around.

Between two trees by the water, you lie in the hammock reading papers and gently swinging. I stop walking and study you—so calm and relaxed—looking nothing like a billionaire business god with your hair blowing back and your chest bare. I could've never picked you out in a crowd—didn't in fact.

You glace up and meet my eyes. "Are you stalking me?"

"I can only aspire to one day be as good of a stalker as you."

You smirk. "I would say you're too nice, but after putting Joan in her place, I think you just might have it in you after all."

"I'm sorry. I shouldn't have done that." She's your employee, not mine.

You shrug. "She has thick skin. I'm sure she's over it."

"Thick skin from working with you?" I walk toward you, running my palm of the tops of tall grass and flowers.

"It's a requirement. I don't like to worry about offending people."

I reach you and weave my fingers through the rope hammock. "What about the honey?"

You roll your eyes, and I shove the hammock with all

my strength, sending you swinging. "Okay!" You laugh. "I said I'd try for more honey, less vinegar. That's what I'll do."

When the hammock swings back toward me, you grab me around the waist and pull me on top of you. "Hey!" We're both laughing and swinging, and I snuggle in beside you, into the crook of your arm with my head on your chest. "You weren't mad about Beck, were you?"

"Why would I be mad? I have no right to be mad—no claim over you."

The heat from your chest warms my cheek. "You kept squeezing my hand."

"I wanted to remind you I was there."

"You were right beside me."

"He was flirting. You were flirting back."

I push up to look at you. "I was not flirting back. He's our foreman. It would be unprofessional."

Your eyes graze my face—over my cheeks, across my lips, down my neck and back to my eyes. "What if he wasn't the foreman, or anyone working for you?"

"What are you asking me?"

Your lips tighten into a firm line. "Nothing."

"It's something. I can tell." I brush a film of sawdust off your chest. Your muscles contract under my fingers.

Your nose nuzzles into my hair. "Does this mean I get to touch your chest, too?"

"Sure, if you're brushing off sawdust."

"You know I'm going to be up all night thinking of ways

to get you covered in sawdust." Your finger trails down my arm, bringing up goose bumps despite the temperature.

Speaking of tonight… "Where is everyone going to sleep? We should probably get some rooms ready."

"So eager to leave me?" You trail your finger up and down my arm again. "I need to get a domestic out here."

"A domestic? Like a maid?"

"Maid, cook, grounds keeper. I'll tell Joan to place employment ads and we'll start interviewing this week."

"I can handle it. We don't need someone right away."

"I don't want you handling it. You're the boss, not the one scrubbing toilets." You kiss my forehead, then guide it back down onto your chest. "I already miss it being just the two of us out here."

I smile. "It's only been a few hours."

"I know. Maybe we can just leave the place in ruins and make them all go home."

I prop my chin on my hands and glance up at you. "You know you don't want to do that."

You tap the tip of my nose. "No. I guess not." You sigh. "It's so much easier when it's only the two of us. No arguments about past partners. No jealously over potentially flirtatious acts with foremen."

"You mean no real life."

"Exactly."

"You're dangerously close to becoming a hermit."

"I told you, I'm considering it. I wasn't joking."

I scowl and put one foot on the ground, tugging your hand. "Come on."

You wrap your arms around me and pull me back down, possessing me with your mouth on mine. Your tongue grazes my bottom lip. I open my mouth and sigh into yours, meeting your tongue with mine. My fingers fist in your hair. I can't get you close enough.

You wrap a hand around the back of my knee and hike my leg up over your hip. I feel the familiar long, thick ridge behind your zipper. You grind it into me. I gasp and run my tongue down onto your neck. You're sweet, like sweat... and honey. "Please don't keep me like this," you groan.

"You said you'd be patient." You grind into me again and I moan.

"You want this, too." Another thrust.

"I do. I can't. Please."

"Please what, Rachael?" Your hands press into my behind as your hips rise and circle.

"Oh. God." I'm losing myself to the delicious heat your body's inflicting. I tug on your bottom lip with my teeth.

"Don't deny yourself. You can have me. Right now." Your hands squeeze and press as your hips rise and circle again.

I'm a senseless, pulsing, aching need. "Please," I beg.

"Please what? You have to tell me. You have to take what you want." You flip us, so now you're on top, and thrust against me. Your breath is hot on my neck, sending tingles down my back. Your moan is irresistible in my ear. "Tell me." Your tongue flicks my earlobe, then you take it in your mouth, sucking.

Your strong body on top of mine increases the heat between my legs, the throbbing, the wetness. You press up on your arms, holding yourself over me. Your eyes burn with need. "Why are you holding back from me?"

"I don't know," I whimper. "I wish I could give in. I want you."

Your hand runs up and down my thigh. "I know you do. I can hear it. I can see it."

"That has to be enough for right now." I close my eyes, not able to stand the disappointment in yours.

Your forehead lowers to rest against mine. We're still and silent, breathing each other's air. "Okay," you whisper. "I'll have to work with this. I'll find a way." It's like you're talking to yourself instead of me. Finding a battle plan for some business takeover. You sit up on your knees and pull me up into a hug. "Let's go back and clear out rooms for the crew to sleep in."

On our way back, your arm never strays from around my shoulders. You're going to be patient, and that's the best honey you can give me.

Eleven

We work in separate rooms, and it's probably for the best or we might not get anything done otherwise. I find nothing to salvage, only old junk and trash to be tossed out. I wonder what we'll do with trash on the island, it's not like there's a trash truck that will rumble down the road every Tuesday morning like at home. Guess we'll have to burn it.

The tell-tale click-clack of heels alerts me to Joan's presence behind me. "Where's Merrick?"

"Not in here." I don't bother turning around.

"The crew has a bonfire going. They're cooking out, brats and beer, so there's no need to fix them anything for dinner."

"Great." Is she expecting me to cook for her? Not likely. "Hope they can sleep a few to a room. Not many of the floors are stable enough to let them use the guestrooms." Out of the twenty rooms, the wood floors were rotted in over half.

"I think they'd rather sleep outside. They brought tents and everything. At least until the hotel is renovated. It's kind of like a guys' retreat out there."

Her light tone makes me turn around and find her smiling. "Sounds like they're having fun."

"They are." Her gentle expression falters. "Do you mind if I take one of the rooms inside?"

Why would she assume I'd have an issue with that, like I'd make her sleep out on the patio or something? "Of course! I expected you to."

She nods. "Have you looked at the clothes I brought you yet?"

"Oh, I forgot about them." I wave a hand around the room. "I got busy."

"It's been an interesting day." She shakes her head and her eyes snap into clear, driven, Dragon Lady focus. "I'll find Merrick."

"You do that," I say as she strides from the room, our fleeting moment of neutrality gone with a rush of her red sundress.

About a half hour later, I finish sorting through the room I'm working in and decide there's no reason to start on another if the men are sleeping outside anyway. My stomach rumbles, but I need a hot shower before anything else.

Jogging down the stairs, I notice my bags are no longer in the kitchen. They must've been moved. I turn and go up to your room—our room?—and find you sitting on the couch looking contemplative. "Something wrong?"

You give me a brief smile and open your mouth to say something, but my phone rings sitting on the coffee table. We both stare at it like it's a bomb threatening to destroy the bubble of denial we've created and survived in the past few days.

"Are you going to answer it?" you ask. Your voice is controlled and quiet. I can't tell what you're feeling.

I don't know, so I don't answer you. My hands are gripped tightly together and pressed into my waist, like touching my phone will burn me worse than the hot casserole dish.

Slowly, you lean forward, pick up the phone and hold it out to me. "Take it. You should answer."

Are you testing me? I probe your eyes for any indication of what you're thinking, but they're as unwavering and controlled as your voice. This must be your business-god-poker-face.

My hand trembles as I reach out and take the phone on its third ring and press the green answer button. "H-hello?" I stutter, watching you lean your elbows on your knees and lower your face into your hands waiting for the bomb to drop.

"Rachael, why didn't you call me back? I left you a message." My mother uses her typical condescending tone. "I was worried."

"You don't need to worry about me."

Your hands drop away from your face, and your eyes go wide watching me.

"How's your trip?" I ask.

"Well, it's rained the past two days, so I'm hoping it doesn't keep up the entire time." Leave it to my mother to be unappreciative of a free multi-week, European vacation.

"It's lovely, Rachael," my aunt calls from somewhere

near my mom. I'm on speaker. "Tell Mr. Rocha thank you. It's a very generous thing to do."

"Well, of course it's generous!" my mom says, like she's been accused of being ungrateful. "I just hope it stops raining so we can take advantage of his generosity."

"How's the consulting coming along?" my aunt asks.

"It's going well." I say, watching your deer-in-headlights expression ease a bit. "There's a work crew here starting renovations. It'll be incredible when it's finished."

"Will you be home soon?" Mom asks. There's an edge to her voice. She's never been alone in her life. She lived with my grandparents until she married my dad. The past year without him has been a trying experience for her—and for me. She expects me to stop by every single day. I don't have my own life. I pay rent to live in an apartment I never spend time in.

"I'll be back when you are."

You sit up straight and hold your hand out to me. I take it and sit beside you.

"You're not very talkative," Mom says. "There's something wrong. I know you." Oh no. She's going to start prying. This I *don't* need.

"Nothing's wrong. I'm just tired. It's been a long day."

You run a hand up and down my back.

"What time is it there?" I ask her. "It has to be late. And where are you?"

"We're just getting ready for bed. We're on the cruise ship heading toward Italy."

"Italy. Wow."

You wrap an arm around me and pull me to you. "I'd like to take you to Italy," you whisper in my ear.

"We'll bring you some pizza," my aunt says, laughing.

"Sounds good. I'm starving."

"I'll make you something." You squeeze my thigh and stand.

"How are you living on that island?" Mom asks as I watch you leave the room. "Does it have any modern conveniences at all?"

"Yes, mom. Merrick—Mr. Rocha—made some updates, like the kitchen and bathroom, so we're able to live comfortably while renovating."

"Merrick, huh?" my aunt says. I don't miss the innuendo in her voice. "First name basis?"

"Well, we are here working together. You normally do call your co-workers by their first names." I will not fall into this trap.

"Co-worker? Isn't he your boss?" Mom says.

"I'm actually the boss on this project." I sound smug. I can't help but smile. I'm the boss.

"I thought you were only consulting." Mom's voice is panicked. "Did you take the project manager position and not tell me?"

"No." Or did I? I really don't know how I got the role of boss other than you gave it to me.

"Then I don't understand this. How can you be the boss?"

"I don't know, Mom. Okay? It just is what it is."

"Stop pestering her," my aunt says. "She's doing what she loves, and she's apparently doing a good job of it. Be happy for her."

"I *am* happy for her." But Mom doesn't sound happy at all. "And I'm proud of you, Rachael. You must be doing a great job if Mr. Rocha put you in charge."

A spike of warmth jolts through my heart. My mom has never said she's proud of me. "Thanks."

After an awkward pause, I make an excuse to get off the phone. "Well, I need to get in the shower and find something to eat. I'm glad you're having a good time. Let me know how Italy is."

"I'll call you in a couple of days. Don't work yourself to death. Stay hydrated. It has to be excruciatingly hot there."

"It is. Don't worry, Mom."

"I love you, Rach."

"Love you, too, Mom."

We hang up, and I set my phone back on the coffee table. Our conversation seemed so normal. I didn't even have to lie to her about how I got here. Maybe we are past that.

I'm still not sure I can touch you, or let you touch me, that I can give you that part of me. You've given me control of the renovations and control over us and if our relationship progresses, so why can't I let go? Why do I still feel vulnerable to you if I hold all the control?

Because what if I let go and then you take it back? The

attraction I feel for you...It would destroy me. I'm afraid of what you could do to me if I give myself over physically—if I give myself emotionally. The two go hand-in-hand with me.

I love the way it feels when I'm close to you, when you nuzzle your nose in my hair, the warmth of your chest against my cheek, your hand squeezing mine. I love seeing unexpected emotions in your beautiful dark eyes.

I might as well give it all up. I'm already gone over you.

On my way to the bathroom, I pass Joan wrapped in a fluffy, white towel. Her golden skin glistens with water. We acknowledge each other with slight smiles and keep walking.

The bathroom is steamy, the mirror fogged. I wipe a towel over it and notice how tan I've become since I got here. My hair's a little lighter, too. I haven't even been outside that much. It must've happened when we were on the water fishing.

I shower, and even though there's brand new body wash and shampoo sitting beside yours, courtesy of Joan, I still use your soap. I like to smell like you. I like everything about you. Maybe tonight...Maybe I'll surprise you.

After my shower, I open the drawer of the dresser at the end of the bed where I normally find your t-shirts. But it's filled with lacy underwear and bras. Each drawer is filled with women's clothing—shorts, shirts, socks, anything and everything I could ever need during my stay. I give Joan an A plus for being thorough.

I pull on a pair of soft, white shorts over a simple white thong, and I'm surprised at just how short they are. But they're a comfortable cotton jersey material. After selecting an aqua blue tank top that accentuates my tan and brushing out my wet hair, I pad down the stairs in flip flops to find you.

You're striding down the hallway toward the kitchen with a plate of grilled chicken in one hand. "Ready to eat?" you ask. "I borrowed the guy's bonfire. They have a make-shift grill grate out there that they made from scrap metal. Geniuses, I swear. I don't give them enough credit."

"It smells incredible." You must've marinated the chicken breasts. My mouth is watering.

"It does smell good. I'm starving, myself. I thought I'd cut these up and put them over big salads unless you'd rather have them another way."

"A grilled chicken salad sound perfect. What can I do to help?"

"Not a thing. Sit and keep me company." You set the chicken on the island and lean over pressing your nose against my shoulder. "I like smelling me on your skin."

"Your body wash," I clarify, tingling from your touch, your warmth and your words.

"My body wash for now. Maybe just my body later." You lift your head, smiling at my stunned reaction.

"You're being very bold tonight. Put your dimples away." I stick my finger in one, trying to keep my breathing to a normal pace while my heart stutters and pounds in my chest. Maybe later...Yes, maybe so.

You chuckle and turn to the refrigerator. "How about a glass of chilled wine?"

"Sounds good." I take one of the chipped mugs out of the cupboard and hold it out while you pour. "Thanks."

"You're welcome." You pour yourself a cup then start cutting the chicken in strips. "I plan to get you drunk tonight."

"Hasn't that been your strategy every night?" I smile around the rim of my mug.

You put the knife down and raise an eyebrow. "It has. Maybe I need a new tactic. What would you suggest?" You pick up a thin slice of chicken and hold it near my lips, offering it to me.

I open mouth and let you place it on my tongue, closing my lips around your fingers as you take them away. "Mmm…" The chicken is bursting with herbs and lemon. I swallow and take a sip of wine. "I suggest you keep doing what you're doing."

You groan. "I need to up my game. You're killing me. Night and day. You have this look you give me that could make me explode in my pants."

"Just a look? Which look is it?"

Your smile hitches into a smirk. "Like I'd tell you. I don't need you torturing me more than you already do." You let out a huge, embellished sigh. "I'll just have to keep being patient and earning your trust."

I hold your deep, dark eyes in mine. The stubble on your jaw casts a shadow over your face, exaggerating your full lips and defining the angles of your cheekbones. I want to kiss you so badly, I can't stand it. You know, too. I see it in your eyes. You know you're breaking my will. You can see my chest heaving, my breath quickening as my pulse speeds. There's no hiding how my body reacts to you.

"That's the look," you whisper. "The look in your eyes when I know you want me."

I close my eyes and squeeze my fists trying to fight the desire flaring through me. God, your voice, your words, your…everything. I do want you. So, so much.

"Stop." You touch my cheek, and I open my eyes to find you shaking your head slowly from side to side, your dark eyes brimming with desire. "Let it happen."

I tear my eyes from yours and inhale a shaky breath. You tip more wine into my mug. "You think I need more, huh?"

"A lot more." You finish cutting the chicken and take two large bowls filled with mixed greens and vegetables out of the refrigerator. "Want to grab the dressing from the top shelf and follow me out to the patio?"

"Okay." The delicious tension between us ebbs second by second, but still assaults me in tidal waves deep inside. If I'm killing you, I don't know what you think you're doing to me.

The earthy, pungent scent of wood smoke hits me when I step outside. "Makes me want to roast marshmallows."

"I'll put them on the shopping list for Joan."

"Don't forget the graham crackers and chocolate." I set

the salad dressing on the wrought iron patio table and sit in my seat.

"I like the combination of you and chocolate." Your fingertips brush my leg under the table. "The taste of you and chocolate cake is like heaven together."

"I could say the same for you." Your flirty grin makes my empty stomach flutter. "Will you stop making comments like that and let me eat, please?"

An innocent expression steals over your face. "Comments like what?"

I pour some dressing on my salad and pick up my fork. "You know like what."

I take a bite as you chuckle. "I can't help that food tastes better when licked off of your lips." Your hand threads through the back of my hair and cups my neck. "Like this little bit of salad dressing right here." Your open mouth finds the corner of mine, and your tongue sweeps over my lips. You back away, smiling. "They should bottle you."

Your kiss is a match, and I'm ignited. "One meal, Merrick. I'm begging you. Just let me eat one meal. I'm starving."

You throw your head back laughing. "Okay, okay. But eat fast." You pick up your fork, grinning. "I can't be blamed. There's something so erotic about watching you eat."

I almost choke. "Pavlov would've had a field day with you."

You twiddle your fork and lean in closer to me. "You know what he did with the dog? He called that "psychic secretion". You trace my ear with your nose. "That's what I try to do to you since you won't let me touch you."

Oh my God. I'm going to combust. My shoulders fall, my eyes close, my hands drop to my lap. I have no will power over you. I surrender.

"What?" You sound alarmed.

"You're killing me. You say I'm killing you, but you're the one killing me."

You take my shoulders and scoot my chair around, pushing against the leg with your foot. "Then stop resisting. You forgave me, remember? Let this happen between us."

I grip your hands on top of my shoulders. "I want to. You don't understand how powerless you made me feel. I don't want that to happen again. If I let this happen between us, my defenses are down. It would just be me, totally vulnerable to you. I just…I'm not ready for that yet."

"Just you…me," you mumble to yourself before jumping up, looking like you've just had a huge revelation. "Don't move. I'll be right back."

Slumped in my chair, I do my best to collect myself and gather my strength. I can't let you do this to me. I need to stay in control. I might have forgiven you, but you haven't earned my trust yet. I don't know you well enough to sleep with you. I've slept with two men in my life, and I loved both of them. I'm not going to turn into a woman who gives it away to any man who gets me hot and bothered.

God, I sound like my mother. She's probably the reason

I've been such a prude. My college years were wasted while Shannon sampled all the flavors men have to offer.

I push my salad away and lean my forehead on the table. Another meal railroaded by lust. I should market this as a diet plan. Shed unwanted pounds by sexual denial. Smother fat and your sex drive one course at a time.

Why am I doing this to myself? It's torture.

At the sound of your footsteps coming back out onto the patio, I lift my head and can't help feeling shy at the lingering knowledge between us that we're going to be very, very intimate soon. It's only a matter of when.

You stop at my chair and stroke my cheek. "I have an idea. You don't have to touch me or let me touch you. Okay? Come upstairs with me."

I'm frozen in place. "What's your idea?"

Your smile loosens my clenched muscles. "Trust me, Rachael." You take my hands and pull me to my feet. "Come on."

You lead me through the lounge, into the entryway, up the stairs, and into the bedroom. Beside the bed, you cup my face and kiss me, slow at first, teasing and tempting, then delving deeper until we're both gasping and your hands are tugging my head back by my hair, giving your lips access to my neck.

"Take this off." You tug the hem of my tank top. "Please. No touching. I promise."

You step back and I hesitate, but you tilt your head and

give me a smile with a gaze that could melt steel. You're not trying to take advantage of me. I know that.

With a quick tug, my top's off, like pulling off a Band-Aid. It didn't hurt at all. I didn't even flinch.

Your eyes roam over my chest, taking in the pretty, white lace bra Joan picked out. I'm sure hers are much racier. I can't imagine her in white lace.

"You're so beautiful," you whisper, pulling off your shirt, taking me in your arms and kissing me again. Your chest is warm and solid against mine. Big and safe. Your hands run down my back, and your fingers hook in the waistband of my shorts. "Now these."

I take a deep breath. My arms shake. Hell with it. I shove them down and kick them off.

Your hands stay at the small of my back, not daring to move down over my bare bottom. "A thong," you say, nibbling my shoulder. "This is taking a ton of will power for me. You know that, don't you?" You chuckle, sending small waves of heat that tickle and tingle down my back.

You sit on the side of the bed. "Lie down. Please." Both of your hands come up in front of you. "No touching. I promise."

This is all part of whatever crazy idea you have. I'm afraid I'll give in, but not scared enough to stop myself from lying on the bed.

You fan my hair out on the pillow and run your fingers through it. "So soft." You slowly trace a finger from my temple to my chin, down my neck, along my collar bone and down my arm. "I'm going to make you feel what I want to do to you, Rachael. The beautiful release I want to give you if you let me."

"How?" I whisper, but it's barely audible, my throat is so constricted by your words.

You lean over me and kiss me again, deep, aching, needful. I thread my fingers in your hair, crushing the dark waves in my hands. You groan, and I come unhinged. My mouth seeks your skin—your neck, your shoulder, your chest. I'm drowning. There's only one thing that can save me now.

A knock sounds on the door. You pull away, sucking my bottom lip as you go. "This is going to work." I'm not sure if you're trying to convince me or yourself.

Why are you going to the door? Tell whoever it is to go the hell away!

You open it. Joan crosses the threshold wearing nothing but red lace and heels. She gazes up at you through her lashes, a look desperate for approval. "Thanks for this," you say, taking her by the wrist and leading her over to the bed where I'm shifting to sit up and hide my practically naked body.

What the fuck is she doing here?

"Rachael," you say in a voice that could calm a cat skittering on a tin roof, "I asked Joan to join us. She's going to do the touching for me. Okay? Will you try?"

This has to be a bad dream.

I turn my head to the door, to you, to her, to the

window. I seem to be awake, but what the fuck is going on? "You asked her to join us?"

You sit back down and try to ease me back onto the pillow again, but I'm not budging. "Let me be with you like this. Let's try it. It's a step, and I don't have to touch you. You can tell her how you want to touch me, too. She'll be our hands, okay? Try. Please, Rachael. Try."

"But…" It's Joan. What makes you think I want her touching me *there*? I've never let another woman touch me *there*.

"You can trust her to do as I say. You can trust me." You stroke my hair, my shoulders, my back. "Let's try it. If you say stop, we stop."

Joan kneels on the bed, pushing you out of the way. "What would you like me to do first?" she asks you. She straddles my legs and brushes my hair back over my shoulders, but will not look me in the eye. I can't blame her. I'm so humiliated for her. Why would she do this?

"Unhook her bra," you whisper, shifting down to the floor on your knees. You take my hand and kiss my palm, running your tongue up my middle finger while Joan reaches around and unclasps my bra, taking it off and tossing it aside.

You take the tip of my finger in your mouth and groan. "Touch her. Squeeze her breasts."

Before I can stop her, Joan slides her hands up my waist and cups my breasts. Oh…I'm so aware of you watching, sucking, moaning.

"Pretend it's me, Rachael," you whisper.

from any Barnes & Noble Booksellers store for returns of undamaged NOOKs, new and unread books, and unopened and undamaged music CDs, DVDs, and audio books made within 14 days of purchase from a Barnes & Noble Booksellers store or Barnes & Noble.com with the below exceptions:

A store credit for the purchase price will be issued (i) for purchases made by check less than 7 days prior to the date of return, (ii) when a gift receipt is presented within 60 days of purchase, (iii) for textbooks, or (iv) for products purchased at Barnes & Noble College bookstores that are listed for sale in the Barnes & Noble Booksellers inventory management system.

Opened music CDs/DVDs/audio books may not be returned, and can be exchanged only for the same title and only if defective. NOOKs purchased from other retailers or sellers are returnable only to the retailer or seller from which they are purchased, pursuant to such retailer's or seller's return policy. Magazines, newspapers, eBooks, digital downloads, and used books are not returnable or exchangeable. Defective NOOKs may be exchanged at the store in accordance with the applicable warranty.

YOU MAY ALSO LIKE...

Ultimate Book of Drawing
by Barrington Barber

The Boy in the Suitcase (Nina Borg...
by Lene Kaaberbøl

Rising Storm (Bluegrass Brothers Series #2)
by Kathleen Brooks

Fundamentals of Drawing Animals
by Duncan Smith

Midnight on Julia Street
by Ciji Ware

My eyes close, and I let my head fall back. I grab your face, stroke your jaw and insert my thumb into your mouth.

"Nipples," he says.

Joan rolls my nipples between her fingers and thumbs, twisting and tugging. Electricity shoots down my stomach and sizzles between my legs.

"Suck," you say, sucking the end of my thumb, mimicking Joan's lips on my nipple.

"Ah..." I can't believe we're doing this. That some woman—some woman you've been with—is doing this to me.

"Put your hand between her legs," you say. "Rachael, I'm going to make you come."

Joan's hand slides down my stomach. Her fingers slip inside my thong. Your fingers circle against my palm, just like hers circle against—I gasp and push her away. "No. Stop."

It's like waking up from the worst and best dream I've ever had all mixed into one confusing moment. "I can't do this." I push her off of me and slide to the edge of the bed. You stop me, sitting between my knees with your hands on my waist.

"You liked it. I know you did." You're as confused as I am. "Why are you stopping?"

I glance back at Joan. She's gazing out the window. Her eyes are brimming with tears. I feel dirty and like I got talked into doing something I'd never do in a million years. Why did I do this? "This is so wrong."

I stand and push your shoulders so you move out of my way, grab my clothes and dart out of the room.

"Rachael!" You come after me, but I run into the bathroom and lock the door. "Rachael?" You knock softly. "Talk to me. Please."

"There's nothing to talk about." I whisk tears off of my cheeks and tug my shorts on. I'm so embarrassed. And Joan…she'd do anything for you.

My heart clenches. I need to get out of here. I need to go home. I yank my tank top over my head and pull the door open. You're leaning against the jamb, looking stricken, blocking my way.

"I don't understand." You reach out for me, but I step back. Your brow creases as pain crosses your face. "You've been crying. Tell me what I did wrong."

"What you did wrong?" I can't believe your lack of comprehension. "How could you think what just happened is in any way appropriate? If I didn't want you touching me, why in the hell would I want her touching me?"

"But you do want me touching you. You just aren't ready for it. You said if it was just you and me…" You shake your head. "I thought this would be a good way to do it."

My chin drops to my chest. This is just like your other relationship problems. "You don't have any idea how you take other people's feelings for granted." I'm desolate. Empty. You did it to me, before I could help you fix things with Heidi, before I could make you understand. You did it to me, too.

"I did think of you! All I was thinking about was how you would feel. How I could make this work between us in a way that wouldn't push you. I didn't touch you, Rachael! You can't be mad about this!"

I was stupid to think I could fix you. "I'm leaving in the morning. I'll ask Joan to arrange it."

"No." You pull at your hair then pound your fist against the doorframe. "Don't go. Don't leave me."

"I can't stay. Not after this." I brush by you, and you wrap an arm around my waist, pulling me back against you.

You don't say anything, just lean your head against mine. Your heart pounds against my back, like a frightened child. You take a shaky breath and squeeze me tighter, with both arms now.

I hate myself for wanting to stay here, for wanting to turn and take you in my arms and hold you as tight as you're holding me. To stroke your face, your hair, your back and tell you it's okay. That I know you didn't mean any harm to me or to Joan. I hate that I have to walk away. "Merrick," my voice wavers. "Let me go."

You instantly drop your arms, and I step away.

"I'll tell Joan you're leaving," you say, your head hung, your fingers rubbing your temples.

"You owe her an apology. She's in love with you. I'm not sure you're aware of that. She'd do anything for you—even what she just did to me—to make you happy."

Your eyes rise to mine. "She's not in love with me, Rachael. She's in love with the billionaire, with the status and the money, with thinking she could tell people she's Mrs. Rocha." You roll your eyes up to the ceiling and take a deep breath. "If I wasn't loaded, she wouldn't want anything to do with me." You rub your forehead roughly. "Story of my life."

"Is that why you're talking about giving it all up?"

You nod and slump against the wall, crossing your arms over your bare chest. "I want to be me, not a dollar figure." You follow a snort of derision with a smirk. "I don't even know who that is."

I reach out a trembling hand and touch your cheek. "I do. You'll like him."

You grasp my hand, but I tug it away. "I'll sleep downstairs."

"No. The bed is yours. I won't ever touch it again."

I hurt so badly inside; it feels like we've been together for a lifetime and we're breaking apart. "Goodnight, Merrick."

You open your mouth, but let it close again. Your lips press tight, and you turn and jog down the stairs.

You're hurting.

I'm hurting.

This has gone so wrong so fast.

Twelve

*J*oan hasn't moved from her position on the bed by the window. I'm so embarrassed for both of us, I could die. But I know I have to say something to her.

Easing down on the edge of the bed, I see the tears are no longer in her eyes; they're streaked down her cheeks. "I'm sorry," I say. "That shouldn't have happened."

Her head snaps to face me. "No. It shouldn't have. You shouldn't be such a child."

It's as if she's slapped me. I stand and stare at her, shocked. "A child?"

"That man," she says, pointing to the door, "has never given a shit about anyone but himself. No matter how many women have come and gone and fallen head-over-heels for him, he's never once looked back when he tossed them aside. Then you come along, and his head is so far up your ass he can't even think."

"What?" I blink at her, maybe my ears aren't working.

Joan shoots up on her knees and scoots forward so we're eye-to-eye. "I'd give anything in the world to have Merrick treat me like he does you. To have him want me like he wants you." She sits back on her heels and begins to laugh through her tears. "Jesus, a nobody from Cleveland who didn't even want the job. Now this place is yours."

"This place isn't mine, and I'm leaving in the morning. Is there someone here who can fly me back, or do arrangements need to be made?" I'm sorry she's upset, but I'm not going to stand here and listen to her call me a nobody.

"You're leaving? Just like that? He's laying everything at your feet, and you're leaving."

"Joan, look at what just happened here. That's not giving a shit about anyone but himself. He certainly didn't take your feelings into consideration! How can I stay?"

She glares at me. "You don't get him at all. I'm glad you're leaving. You don't deserve him."

On her feet, and halfway to the door, she stops and turns back to me. "There's someone here to fly you to the airport. I'll have a ticket waiting to take you home. Be at the helicopter at eight A.M."

She slams the door, and I flop back on the bed. How did I end up being public enemy number one in this mess? Am I a tease for not having sex with you? Should I have let go of my apprehensions—shut off my brain—and let you touch me using Joan? Should I have told her to touch you?

Shit. Shannon would've. She would've gotten into it, too. Of course, Shannon doesn't get attached. She can do the sex-without-strings thing. I can't. I've never tried, but I know I can't. There were a few moments when I was kind of getting into it though…

The dull pounding of bass from music outside thrums through my body. I pull the pillow over my face to drown out the sound of the crew having a good time. I wish you and I were out there with them having a good time. But, there's no way back now, only forward to eight A.M. and never seeing you again.

You're gone from my life, my mom's in Europe, and I can't imagine going back to my dull existence. I've never felt so lonely and empty.

I don't see you in the morning before I leave. The hotel is quiet and still, like no other living being is inside. I'm not sure what I'd say to you if I saw you, so it's probably for the best if we don't say goodbye. At least, that's what I tell myself.

Beck Tanner's waiting at the helicopter to fly me to the airport. "Morning," he says, and gives me a shit-eating grin. "Leaving so soon? I thought we'd have you around until the renovation is done."

"Plans changed." I ignore the pang in my chest and the lump in my throat and fasten my harness. Fortunately, Beck doesn't press me to talk more about my departure from Turtle Tear. I don't think I can handle fumbling for words right now.

The propeller gains speed, and Beck makes short work of getting us up in the air. The trees bend and blow, and my eyes catch on the roof of the tree house. My stifled sob sounds deep, metallic and primal through my earphones. I close my eyes and refuse to watch the hotel, the island and my dreams fall away below.

It seems like only minutes have passed when Beck's landing the helicopter on the tarmac of a small, private airport beside a jet with the Rocha Enterprises logo on the side. You have everything and want none of it. You don't even know yourself.

I thought I knew you—not well—but I was wrong. I never could've predicted what you did last night. How can one brilliant man be so oblivious?

"I'll come around for you," Beck says before pulling off his headphones.

I take mine off as well and unhook my harness. He helps me down and leads the way to the jet. I brought nothing with me but the clothes I arrived in, my phone and my wristlet.

"You'll be taken to Cleveland Hopkins Airport. A driver will meet you there to take you home." Beck takes my hand. "I don't know what happened, and I'm not asking. You should know that I've worked for Mr. Rocha for years, and I've never seen him more…" he looks down at his work boots and shuffles his feet, searching for the right word, "normal. Approachable. You cracked some invisible barrier he's always had around him."

I put a hand up. I can't stand hearing this.

"Just know," he continues anyway, tearing me apart with his sincerity, "that you helped. And I don't mean only with the renovation. He came out and pitched in yesterday. Took his shirt off, sawed some wood, joked around. He's happy is what I'm telling you. I don't dare to call him a friend, but if the man I saw yesterday stays around, I'd like to."

"I hope that man stays around." I sniff and run the back of my hand under my nose. "He could use a good friend."

"I hope you come back." He leans in and kisses my cheek. "You know you'll be missed."

I nod and turn around, mumbling my thanks and goodbye.

The jet's big enough for at least twelve people to fly comfortably. There's a pilot, co-pilot and flight attendant just for me. I settle into a soft leather seat by the window and decline a beverage. I don't want to take anything else from you, not even a bottle of water. You're impossible, and I can't give back, so what's the point?

I need to get home and sleep for days, forget any of the past week ever happened.

Unfortunately, when the driver of the black hired Mercedes pulls up at the curb in front of my apartment, Shannon's car is in the driveway. I know she's going to pepper me with questions. "Can I be dropped off somewhere else?" I ask the driver. "If it's a problem, I understand."

He turns and smiles. "Of course it's not a problem. Where to?"

I give him my mom's address, silently thanking you for sending her away. At least I'll get some peace. Twenty-five minutes south on the highway, and we're in the suburb where I grew up. The yellow two-story colonial sits on a quiet street surrounded by neighbors whose kids I grew up with. Many of them are grandparents now.

I want to linger outside, walk through the flower garden and sit on the covered front porch. But the driver keeps watch, waiting for me to open the front door before he pulls away, so I turn the key in the lock and step inside.

Despite the faint scent of lemon polish, the house smells stale, like a forgotten pack of crackers left open on the counter. It's too hot. Mom always turns the A.C. off when we go on vacations. The hum of the refrigerator is reassuring—the house hasn't died and withered while we were gone.

I flip on the A.C., open the blinds and plop down on the old plaid couch to watch mindless T.V. for a while. I can't stop my mind from running in an endless loop of circles, but maybe I can trick it into thinking of something other than you for two minutes.

There's a picture of my dad on the mantle. He's laughing at something beyond the camera's lens. He was an extreme man. He could love, and he could hate in equal capacity. Sometimes he'd flip from one to the other—hot, cold, happy, miserable, laughing, yelling. It was hard to keep up.

When I was young, he and Mom fought a lot. I don't know what they fought about, seems like it could have been anything. He'd yell, and she'd retreat. I'd see her expression change, her eyes darken, like she was closing the shades and barring the windows, turning in on herself until the storm passed. I know she had a hard time being married to him for all those years, but she loved him and they got through the hard times. I wonder if she'd go back and do it all over again, or if she'd take a different path if given the chance.

Nobody's perfect. That's what Mom told me when Lance and I broke up. *Nobody's perfect.*

I guess she's right, but how imperfect is acceptable? Someone who thinks he's making things right by bringing another woman into bed with you? How can I forget that, or forgive it?

It's over now. It doesn't matter. I'll never see you again.

The thought makes my stomach clench and my chest heave, sending tears flowing down my cheeks.

I'll never see you again.

My time with you was a nightmare, then a dream, then a nightmare again. How can you make mistake after mistake? Why does it have to be that way with you? If I want the good, do I have to suffer through the bad? Forgive and forget over and over again?

So much for the distraction of mindless T.V. I was fooling myself to think there was any way to distract myself from thoughts of you, from having this breakdown that's been building for days. The push and pull of my attraction to you, my body battling my brain—something had to give.

Exhausted, with puffy, gritty eyes, all I want to do is sleep forever. I scoot down on the couch, pull an afghan from the back over my legs and let myself drift.

I wake to my phone chiming. It's dark. The T.V.'s chattering away to nobody.

The e-mail icon on my cell's screen shows two new e-mail messages. Shannon would text or call. It's probably junk or spam. I click my inbox anyway, too curious not to look.

The first e-mail is from my internship advisor asking where I've been. I ignore it, not sure how to answer or if I even want to. Hello, opportunity missed. Maybe you didn't think it was a good opportunity, but it's better than what I'm left with—nothing.

The second email address makes me gasp, close my eyes and grit my teeth to suppress the whimper threatening to explode from my throat.

From: MRocha@RochaEnterprises.com
To: RachaelDSalv4@freemail.com
Subject: Turtle Tear Project Going Forward

Ms. DeSalvo,

I've instructed all contractors to reach you via email and your cell number as you have chosen to work remotely on this project.

If you do not wish to have contact with me professionally, please direct communication through Joan, and she'll relay any necessary information between us. I believe you have her email address from when she set up your interview with me.

Regards,

M. Rocha

Regards? Are you kidding me? Why would contractors contact me? I've chosen to work remotely? No. I've chosen to walk away. Why are you so thick headed?

I hit reply intending to nail you against the wall with razor sharp words.

From: RachaelDSalv4@freemail.com
To: MRocha@RochaEnterprises.com
RE: Turtle Tear Project Going Forward—YOU'RE DELUSIONAL

Mr. Rocha,

You misunderstand me. I've left on all terms—personal AND professional. The job is all yours. Emails and phone calls from contractors will be forwarded back to you.

Regards

(Regards? You must regard me as a fool.),

R. DeSalvo

My thumb jams down on the send button. How dare you send contractors my way. I know you're not that stupid. This is your attempt at keeping tabs on me without stalking me like last time.

I toss my phone beside my wristlet and storm into the kitchen to look for chocolate. Then my mind makes the connection between you and chocolate and it's the last thing I want to eat—*ever again.*

I grab a can of Coke from the fridge and slam it shut. Regards. Who uses regards to sign an email? Why does one word make me so angry? Because you had no regard for my feelings last night? Or because you thought you were regarding my feelings but were totally clueless? What a hypocritical word for you to use. Did you select it on purpose to piss me off?

I stuff a handful of potato chips into my mouth and crunch down angrily. With my snack and Coke in hand, I storm back to the couch. It's got to be late. I pick up my phone to check the time. Quarter after eleven. I have a new email message.

After swallowing too quickly, the jagged chips scratching my throat, and taking a gulp of pop, I groan and open your email.

From: MRocha@RochaEnterprises.com
To: RachaelDSalv4@freemail.com
Subject: Fool

Ms. DeSalvo,

I've never thought you a fool. I'm guilty only of thinking of you as a bright, beautiful woman.

You left me, not the hotel. Don't do yourself and Turtle Tear the disservice of walking away from the renovation. You're the only one for the job. We both know that.

Yours,

Merrick

"Very often, say what you will, a knave is only a fool."—Voltaire

Yours. That word makes me even crazier. I was never yours. I couldn't let myself be yours. I couldn't give myself over to you. Who am I angrier with, you or me? I don't know anymore.

If I would've let myself take a risk, last night would have never happened. But it did, and even if it hadn't, you'd do something equally stupid in the future. To be with you is to know hurt and heartache lay in wait ready to ambush and assault my heart.

From: RachaelDSalv4@freemail.com
To: MRocha@RochaEnterprises.com
RE: Fool

I never thought of you as a knave, only an impulsive, misguided man.

I'll think about staying with the project remotely and give you my answer in the morning.

Goodnight,
Rachael

Any contact with you ambushes my heart. A few minutes later, another email pops into my inbox.

From: MRocha@RochaEnterprises.com
To: RachaelDSalv4@freemail.com
Subject: Lonely

I'm a lonely, irrational, misguided man now that you're gone.

Sweet Dreams,
Merrick

I hold my phone to my chest and sob. I don't know where all these tears are coming from. I should be dehydrated by now. My head throbs, and my heart aches. I'm weak and mentally exhausted. Lance and I were together for two years, and I wasn't this devastated when we broke up. You affect me like I've never been affected by another man. It's like I lost part of myself when I left you. You understand me. You said we were alike. We are. We think alike. I just wish we could love alike.

It's seven in the morning, and I've slept like crap. I have no idea if I want to stay on the project or not. Okay, I know I want to, but I don't know if it's because of the project or because of you. Maybe both and that scares me. I need to stay away from you and clear my head.

Talking this through with someone would help, but Shannon would tell me I should go for it, that I was stupid not to sleep with you on day one, and have a plane ticket in my hand before I could object.

My mom—not an option. She can't be unbiased when it comes to me, or unselfish. She'd have me living in my old bedroom already if I gave in to her constant badgering.

Aunt Jan would be good to talk to, but how do I get her on the phone without Mom knowing and butting in?

I dial her number and when she picks up, I cut her off before she can speak. "Don't say who's on the phone. Did you tell Mom already when you saw the number?"

"Uh...no."

"Good. I need to talk to you, but I don't want her knowing about it. Can you find a time to call me when she's not around?"

"She's in the shower right now, Rachael. What's going on? Are you okay?"

I let out a sigh of relief and lean back in my chair at the kitchen table. "I'm fine. I have...man problems and need someone to talk to."

She laughs. "All men are problems. What's this one done? And let me guess, Merrick?"

"Yes. How'd you know? I thought I threw you off that trail." I smile. My aunt has always had a way of knowing what's going on with me.

"A man does not shell out the cash Mr. Rocha did to send a girl's mother and aunt on a cruise to get her alone unless he intends to make a move. I'm guessing it's that move that you're having second thoughts about?" I hear the amusement in her voice.

I pound my fist on the oak table. "He's so frustrating. You can't imagine. I didn't even agree to run this project—not really, not that I remember saying in so many words—but somehow he got me to do it. I find myself going along with him and then wondering what happened, like I was in some kind of haze or something."

"Love does that to you," she says, laughing. "Or lust. You can be the judge of which you're feeling."

"Maybe a little of both. Or a lot of one and some of the

other. I don't know. That's just it. I can't come to terms with how I feel about him." For reasons I can't divulge to anyone.

"Well, there are obviously reasons why you can't come to terms with how you feel. Do you know what those reasons are?"

I knock on the table with my knuckles. "Yes."

"Are they valid, or based on irrational fear?"

"Irrational fear?" I lean forward.

"Yes, irrational fear. Nobody falls in love without running the risk of getting hurt. It's irrational though if you trust the other person not to hurt you. Do you trust him?"

"No. Not yet. I don't know if I ever could."

"Then your fear is valid. Don't give your heart away to someone you can't trust, Rachael."

I close my eyes and lean back again. "I know. I wish... I wish I could trust him. He doesn't hurt me intentionally. He's just so *stupid* when it comes to feelings. He does things that he thinks will make me happy, but destroy me instead. He doesn't get it."

"Sounds like a lack of communication, not so much that he's intentionally hurting you. Can you teach him to communicate?"

"I was going to try, but I left."

"You left? You're home?"

"Who's home?" my Mom's voice shrills over the line from somewhere in the room.

"I'm sorry," Aunt Jan whispers. "Rachael's home. She's not sure how long though."

"Did something happen?" Mom's panicked.

"No, she—"

"Let me talk to her." There's scrambling with the phone. "Rachael?" Mom says. "Are you okay?"

"I'm fine, Mom. No need to worry." I rub my aching forehead. This is exactly what I wanted to avoid.

"Did something happen with Mr. Rocha?"

"No, Mom. I just came home to get some clothes." Why am I saying this? I'm not going back.

"How long are you staying?"

"I fly back tomorrow." I cringe. I hate lying to her.

"Oh. Well, have a safe trip. Call when you get there."

"I will. Tell Aunt Jan goodbye for me."

When we hang up, I lay my head on the table. This situation is so ridiculous. There's nothing left for me here. I have no job, an apartment and roommate I'm avoiding, and I'm lying to my mom. I don't want to be here or there with you, but there's no door number three at the moment.

I'm lying to myself, too. I do want to be there with you, but I can't be. Even Aunt Jan said it—I can't be with someone I don't trust. Can I teach you? I don't know. Will you devour me, my heart, and my emotions before you learn?

It feels like I'm circling a fire, debating on whether to pounce into the flames or not. People don't dive into flames unless they're stupid. I'm not stupid, but I'm acting stupid. You're making me act stupid.

Ugh. I bang my head gently against the table. The ping of an email alert on my phone has my head popping up.

From: MRocha@RochaEnterprises.com
To: RachaelDSalv4@freemail.com
Subject: Decisions

Rachael,

I did a lot of thinking last night. I apologized to Joan. I'd like to make it up to you

somehow.

Apologies are far more effective in person though.

Hope to see you soon,

Merrick

Good luck with that. I'm not going back.

From: RachaelDSalv4@freemail.com
To: MRocha@RochaEnterprises.com
RE: Decisions

Merrick,

I haven't made up my mind. There's a lot to take into consideration.

You've already apologized. What's done is done.

Indecisive,

Rachael

After sending off my reply, I lay my head back down on the table. My stomach growls. I need food, but Mom made sure to clean out the fridge before leaving for three weeks. If I had the energy, I'd go out and get something.

My phone rings. It's Shannon. I can't bring myself to talk to her, so I let it go to voicemail. Then I send her a text letting her know I'm home and at my mom's, and I'll stop by the apartment later today. I feel terrible avoiding her.

I wander into Mom's room hoping to find a book to read. After perusing her bookshelf for a while, I pick a memoir that looks like it has zero romance and crash on her bed to read. I get three pages in when there's a knock on the front door.

I should've never told Shannon I was here. Now she'll pester me to get out of my ratty old bathrobe and do something with my hair and go shopping. Maybe she'll want to go to lunch though. I'm still ready to chew my fingers off. I should order Chinese.

I grab the doorknob and yank the door open. "I knew you'd show up."

She's looking sexy as always in a black halter top and jean shorts. Her golden blonde hair is pulled up in a high ponytail, her skin is bronzed to perfection and I'm left wondering how we ever became friends we're so completely opposite. She whips her sunglasses off and looks me up and down. "You look like shit."

"I feel like shit." I stand back and let her inside.

"So, what the hell happened to you?" She plops down on Mom's couch, picks up a magazine from the coffee table and crosses her legs. I sit next to her. "Last thing I knew," she says, flipping through the celebrity rag magazine, "I left you at the club eyeing up some hot piece of man meat. Then you disappear, and I get a call from some woman telling me you're in Florida doing work on that hotel project you turned down. How'd that happen?"

"I...well, it's...wait. How did you get your car?"

She shakes her head. "What the hell are you talking about? You left it in the driveway."

Merrick must've taken care of that, too.

"Rachael? Hello?" She snaps her fingers in front of my face. "Something's going on with you." She swivels to face me. "What happened?"

I rub my arms and try to think of a way to start this conversation. "You know the man meat? That was Merrick Rocha."

She stares at me blank-faced.

"Of Rocha Enterprises. You know, the billionaire businessman who offered me a job?"

"Oh!" She cocks her head and gives me a strange look. "He's not old."

"No. He's not. Anyway, we left for Florida that night and that's where I've been. At the hotel on Turtle Tear Island in the Everglades."

Her eyebrows shoot up and she clucks her tongue. "Alone with the billionaire? Is he a sex god, too?"

I can't help the sigh that falls through my lips. "I wouldn't know. It's...complicated."

She grabs my shoulders and shakes me. "Rachael. He's hot as hell. What's complicated about that?" Her hands drop. "He's married."

I laugh. If only that were the problem, our relationship would be cut and dry—friends only. "No. He's not."

"Gay?"

"Not even close."

"Then there's something wrong with you, cuz the man I saw at the club had a serious body and a face that could soak panties from here to hell and back. *What* is the problem?" She tosses the magazine onto the table and leans back folding her arms. "I know you're not saving it all up for marriage. That cherry's been popped. So, what is it?"

I grimace. "Do you have to talk like that?"

She waves her hand at me. "We're not in middle school."

"I told you, it's complicated. And it's over, so whatever."

She takes my hands and swings them back and forth between us. "What happened? Tell your bestest friend in the world what happened."

Her sing-song voice cracks me open. Sobs break from my throat. Tears lurch from my eyes. "I can't talk about it. He...he..." I gasp for air. "He's so stupid!"

She laughs. "Of course he's stupid. He's a man. They're all stupid. That's why we're here—women were put on earth to smack some sense into them. They think with their dicks. We're their brains."

I sob and sniffle some more. "I don't want to have to tell him how to act. He should know these things...the things he does...he hurts me."

"Does he hit you?" She jumps off the couch. "I'll kick his ass. I'll get a whole gang of guys to kick his ass!"

"No!" I grab her hand and pull her back down on the couch. "He thinks he's doing nice things that I'll like, but...

gah! I can't explain it." I wipe my eyes on the sleeve of my robe.

She twists her lips in annoyance. "Well, you're being a little vague. Maybe it you actually told me something it would help."

I lick my lips and rub them together before blurting, "He brought another woman to bed with us the night I decided I was going to have sex with him."

Shannon is speechless. She sits and stares at me, blinks a couple times. "That's never happened to me."

I'm not sure if she says it for comparison's sake, or if she honestly has no idea how to respond. "First time for me, too."

"What did you do?" She leans forward and folds the collar of my robe, straightening it.

"Nothing at first. I went along with it. Until things got a little too...personal. Then I ran out of the room and locked myself in the bathroom."

"Was it—what was it like?" She bites her nail.

"I don't know!" I stand up and take a few paces to the window. "It didn't last long. I freaked and ran out."

"Huh."

When I turn and look at her, she's still biting her nail. "What?"

"I've always wondered what I'd do in that situation, but somehow it's never come up. I'm kind of surprised it happened to you first."

"Jesus," I mutter, and turn back to the window. It's bright out, looks hot. Not as hot as Turtle Tear. I wonder what you're doing right now, how the renovations are going today.

"How'd it end?"

I spin around. "I left. I told him I couldn't deal and ran."

She shrugs a shoulder. "Seems a little drastic. I mean, he's kinky, so what?"

I shake my head. "No. No, it's more than that. I told you, it's complicated. You just have to take my word for it. It can't work out."

Shannon stands and holds her arms out. "Okay, I believe you. Come here."

I cross the room and she pulls me into a big hug. "My heart hurts."

"I know. I know it does." She pats my back. "What you need is a few cosmopolitans and new sexy underwear."

"I'd rather have ice cream and sweatpants."

"No, no, no." She takes my arms and backs up a step. "You want back on that wagon, but you don't want it to buckle under your weight." She hooks an arm around me and leads me to the bathroom. "Shower and change. We're drinking and shopping and by tonight you won't remember his name."

I take a shaky breath and blow it out. "Okay." Before I shut the bathroom door, I turn to her. "How's Seth, or Shane or what's-his-name that you met at the club?"

"Who?" She smirks and giggles. "Over. He has no idea what to do with that thing between his legs. Which is unfortunate, because it's a nice one."

I roll my eyes and shut the door, thinking about how nice yours is. Too bad I'll never get to know how well you use it.

Thirteen

I'm so drunk I can't see straight.

"One more," Shannon urges. "Don't be a pussy."

"I can't feel my tongue." The words seem to echo somewhere inside my head. I'm not sure I said them aloud.

She laughs though, so I guess I did. "Do you remember his name?"

"Yeah. Shitface." I laugh so hard, my elbow slips out from under me, sending my head, which was perched on my hand, lurching toward the bar. It hits, but I don't feel anything.

"Rach!" Shannon tugs me up off the bar. "That had to hurt like hell."

"I'm numb." I laugh again.

"She's not driving, right?" The bartender eyes me like I'm his one-way ticket to jail. He has nice blue eyes. Unlike your brownish-black ones that drill straight through mine.

"Shitface," I say again. "He's such a shitface."

"No," Shannon tells the bartender. "She's not driving. Can I get a cup of ice?"

He sits the ice down and she wraps some in a napkin and holds it to my forehead. "He really did a number on you, huh?"

"Who?" I pluck an ice cube out of the glass and suck on it. "Shitface."

"I love Shitface, and I hate him. Mostly, I want to fuck him."

"Hey!" She jolts her head back in surprise. "Did that just come out of your mouth, Rachael DeSalvo?"

"Hell yeah it did." My head starts aching through the numbness making my train of thought derail. "Ouch." I press my fingers against the cold, wet skin under the napkin Shannon's holding.

"Let's get you home, nympho."

I laugh and then cringe. "I think my head's swelling."

The drive home is a blur. Shannon tugs me out of the car and shoves me in the door of our apartment where I crash on the couch. My phone chirps, but I ignore it. My fingers wouldn't be able to function to answer it anyway.

"Here. Hold this to your head." She hands me a plastic zip-lock bag filled with ice. "How do I stop this thing from driving me crazy?" She's pressing buttons on my phone.

"Throw it against the wall. Who cares?" My mom's face travels through my consciousness long enough to be irritating, then your face does. "Shitface," I mumble. Then I close my eyes and focus on breathing and not puking.

I wake up on the couch with my stomach rolling and lurching and make a mad dash for the bathroom. After puking my stomach inside-out, I notice the giant, black and blue goose egg in the middle of my forehead. "Shannon!"

She mutters something from behind her closed bedroom door. I shove it open and throw myself down on her bed. "What the hell happened to my head?"

She opens one eye. "You got drunk and whacked it on the bar."

"How did that happen? I don't remember anything." I'm having an eerie déjà vu moment of another night I ended up blacking out.

"You were drunk, Rach. No big deal. You had fun." She turns away and stuffs a second pillow over her head. "Now leave me alone until at least eleven."

I push her shoulder and stand to leave. "Hey," she says, "your phone's on my nightstand."

I grab it and don't think anything of it until I see the light flashing with a new message in my inbox. I try not to look at it as I make coffee in the kitchen, but fail. When I go to my inbox, there are several messages between you and me from last night. My heart stops for a few seconds. I don't remember sending you any emails last night. Shit. What did I say? The first two are from you:

From: MRocha@RochaEnterprises.com
To: RachaelDSalv4@freemail.com
Subject: Can we talk?

Rachael, I'd like to talk. Is this a good time to call?

From: MRocha@RochaEnterprises.com
To: RachaelDSalv4@freemail.com
Subject: Not a good time?

Since I haven't heard from you, I'll try to get in touch tomorrow.

I miss you, Rachael.

From: RachaelDSalv4@freemail.com
To: MRocha@RochaEnterprises.com
Subject: I'm an idiot.

I got drunk off my ass tonight and talked about you non-stop. My best friend thinks I'm stupid for not screwing your brains out, and if I don't tell you how I feel, she's going to drag me back to that hotel by my hair.

Oh. My. God. I did not write this. "Shannon! I'm going to kill you!"

The lock on her bedroom door clicks. "You'll thank me someday."

"Shit! I can't believe you did this to me!"

"Read them all."

From: MRocha@RochaEnterprises.com
To: RachaelDSalv4@freemail.com
RE: I'm an idiot.

I'm guessing if Rachael's that drunk then this is from the best friend, Shannon. Is that right? Is she okay? What did she say? I want her back here as much as you do. More. How do I get her to come back to me?

From: RachaelDSalv4@freemail.com
To: MRocha@RochaEnterprises.com
RE: I'm an idiot.

Quit doing stupid shit that freaks her out. She's not that kind of girl. She doesn't have sex to have sex. If she loves and trusts you, she'll be with you. So earn her trust.

From: MRocha@RochaEnterprises.com
To: RachaelDSalv4@freemail.com
RE: I'm an idiot.

HOW??? I'll do anything. I need her.

From: RachaelDSalv4@freemail.com
To: MRocha@RochaEnterprises.com
RE: I'm an idiot.

That's for you to figure out, but don't give up. She has real feelings for you. She needs you too. Get her back there somehow.

From: MRocha@RochaEnterprises.com
To: RachaelDSalv4@freemail.com
RE: I'm an idiot.

I'll do everything I can to prove to her how much I need her here with me. She's all I need. Take care of her tonight.

Merrick

"Well?" Shannon calls from her room.

I squeeze my eyes against the tears trying to overflow out of them. I'm not sure what hurts worse, my head or my heart. "What can I say? You told him, and he's going to do whatever he can...whatever that means."

I toss my phone on the counter and slump against it. Shannon's bare feet pad down the hall. She peeks around the kitchen doorway. "Are you pissed at me?"

I take in her messy bed-head and smudged mascara and laugh. "No. How could I be pissed at you? You were only trying to help."

"Maybe I did." She shuffles over to me with her arms out wide and I fall into them. "It's going to work out, I know it."

"I'm glad one of us can be confident about it." I step back and rub my eyes. "I'm going to jump in the shower. Then I need to run back to my mom's and turn her A.C. off. If I forget, she'll kill me when she gets home."

Shannon tugs the refrigerator door open. "Ah, the exciting life of Rachael DeSalvo. The drama never ends." I play-kick her in the butt and she spins around laughing. "Don't forget some cover-up on that big ugly on your forehead you lush."

Mom's house is so quiet and inviting, that I find myself lying on my old bed staring at the patterns of light that cross my ceiling streaming in over the top of my closed blind. I can almost make my mind go blank lying here in silence tracing the lines and angles over and over with my eyes.

I'm almost in a trance when there's a knock at the door. The knock sounds again. I slide off my bed glancing at the clock, realizing it's when the mail comes. I stride out of my room to the front door, fling it open and look directly into your piercing dark eyes.

You drop your hand, mid-knock. "Hi."

I'm frozen in shock. "You're here."

"I'm here. This wasn't the first place I looked though. You must be in hiding. Shannon gave up your location. Don't be too mad at her. I can be pretty persuasive."

"And charming," I say, remembering your words when you told me you spoke to my mom.

Instinctively, I raise my hand to touch your untypically smooth face, but pull it back before I touch you.

"I shaved." Your smile is too much to bear. You look so much younger without your stubble, so innocent.

"What are you doing here?" My words are weak, a breathy whisper from a desperate woman.

"I told you if I had a chance to do everything over, I'd show up at your door and ask you to go get coffee. That's what I'm doing. Would you like to go get coffee with me and start over? The right way this time?" You swallow and there's fear in your eyes. If I say no, it'll pain you.

"I-I…" I don't know. I hold up a finger. "Give me a moment."

You nod, and I close the door and lean against it. I can't catch my breath. You're here.

You're here!

I'm pathetic. I can hardly contain myself. I want to open the door and jump into your arms, smother your mouth with my kiss. The debate is over...if there ever really was a debate in my mind at all.

You knock on the door, startling me. I open it to your face full of confusion, anguish and sorrow. "I shouldn't have come. I'm sorry. You wanted to get away."

"No!" I touch my throat, feeling flush with emotion. "No. I'm glad you came. We can start over."

You take a deep breath and exhale through a glorious smile. "Thank God. I thought I'd done it again."

"No. You were a better judge of my feelings this time than I was."

You take my hand away from my neck and kiss my palm. "I can't tell you how sorry I am, Rachael. I didn't mean to hurt you. That was the furthest from my mind— opposite actually, from what I was thinking."

Your lips are so soft and warm on my hand. I run the pad of my thumb over your bottom lip before taking it away. "I know. We can talk more."

You take my hand and lead me down the sidewalk to your car in the driveway. It's not the Mercedes or BMW that I'd expect you to drive. It's a Ford S.U.V.

We're starting over in an unpretentious way with coffee.

Just us. Without expectations.

Fourteen

After helping me into the S.U.V., you come around and get in behind the wheel. "Hi," you say, holding out a hand to me. "I'm Merrick Rocha."

I take your hand. "Rachael DeSalvo."

Your lips brush the back of my hand. "It's a pleasure to meet you. I enjoyed our phone conversation immensely."

I laugh, and your eyes flash with the brilliance of your smile. "Turtle Tear holds a special place in my heart, Mr. Rocha. Do you know how it got its name?"

"Something about Ponce de León being a cheating bastard and turtles laying eggs if I remember correctly. Of course, that's not what they teach you about him in middle school."

My chest swells with our familiarity, recalling one of our first conversations about the hotel. "No, it isn't what they teach you."

You squeeze my hand and back out of the driveway. "I have so much to learn from you, Rachael."

"I'm afraid you might not be an attentive student. You're rather set in your ways."

You pull to the side of the road in front of my mom's house and turn to me. "Your leaving was a huge wake up call for me." You run your hand through your hair. "I don't want to lose whatever this is between us before it even starts." You gesture between us, your lips pressed tight, your dark eyes burning and focused. "I don't know where we end up, but it feels like something important. Something special, life altering. I can't chase you away before we get there." You pull me against you and kiss my cheek. "I'll learn. I'll listen. I'm in your hands, Rachael."

The way your deep, soft words linger in my ears makes me want to curl up against you and never let go. "I'll do my best to help you understand my feelings. I can't promise anything. You know that, right?"

"I'm not asking for promises." You tip my chin up and kiss me gently, chastely. "Not yet."

You pull away from the curb and drive, and I point out the turns to take to the nearest Starbucks. Talk of future promises should make me leery, but you've been so certain of me from the start. What if you've made me into some ideal in your head that I can't live up to? I can't fix you. I can't even stand up to my own mother. How can I possibly think about helping you when I can't help myself?

This is going to be a disaster—*we* are going to be a disaster. One of us weak and insecure, the other fucked up and emotionally, detached searching for a life-line. I don't have a life-line for you, but if I tell you that, you'll tell me I'm wrong. That you know I do, that you heard it in my voice that first time we spoke, that we're so much alike and I can teach you how to think of others first. I know all of your ideas pertaining to us, and there's no changing your mind.

Glancing over at your beautiful, handsome, stubborn

face, I don't want to change your mind. If you didn't believe I was the one who can make a difference in your life, you wouldn't have come for me. I need you to always come for me and make me believe we can work. I don't want to let go of you. I need to know where we go from here, how we end—if we end.

You park and help me down from the S.U.V. Inside, I find a table while you stroll up to the counter to order my mocha latte and whatever you're getting. I can't help but to stare at you, your round, firm backside, your strong thighs shifting under your jeans, narrow waist and hips, broad shoulders, wavy brown-black hair. Confidence and sexuality emanate from your body with every movement. God knows I feel it, the magnetic pull my body responds to, making me burn and yearn for you and dismiss any red flag that waves in my path warning me away.

I can't stay away. I'm a drowning woman. The only way to survive is to hold on to you and ride this out, praying the waves that take us under lift us up again.

You turn and stride toward our table with two lidded paper coffee cups. It's shocking to see you here—in Starbucks—with me. Why would you want me? You could have any woman in the world.

Suddenly, I feel so small and insignificant. On the island, when it was only us, we were equals. I wasn't a newly graduated, unemployed nobody. Back in real life though, I'm invisible and you're a bright flash of white lightning, rich, successful and incredibly attractive.

You set the coffee on the table and sit across from me, studying my face. "What are you thinking?" Your fingers begin drumming beside your cup.

"I just realized something, that's all." I watch your fingers, because I can't look into your eyes.

"What?"

On the edge of my seat, I take a small sip of steaming coffee, hoping the warmth will calm my knotted stomach. "In the real world, we have nothing in common. We don't belong together."

You throw your body back in the chair, chuckling. "Nothing in common, huh? What should we have in common?" I slowly raise my eyes to yours and catch your amusement. "Should we both own real estate in seventeen countries? Should we both be recent grad students? Should we have all the same favorite movies? Tell me what we should have in common."

Shame surges through me. "Lesson number one: Don't belittle my feelings. You're pushing me away by laughing at me."

You jolt forward and grab my hands on top of the table. "I wasn't laughing at you. I'm sorry. I didn't mean to belittle your feelings. I honestly want to know why you think we don't belong together."

"Because you're you! I'm struggling to figure out who I am and what I'm going to do with my life, and you're on top of the world already. I don't belong up there with you, and you definitely don't belong down here with me."

You scowl. "Down here with you? Why are you talking about yourself like you're worthless? If anything, I'm the one who is beneath you." You let go of one of my hands to drag yours through your hair. "We didn't have this problem until right now. Why has the power shifted all of the sudden? Why are you looking at me like I'm God instead of the asshole who . . . stole you away?"

I bite the inside of my cheek and feel the wall between us thickening. "Because we started over."

You shake your head and stare at me with an incredulous look on your face. "You'd rather have the asshole who drugged you? He's down on your level, is that what you think? You think you deserve how I treated you?"

"No! Of course not. But we started out with you proving yourself to me, not the other way around."

You take a deep breath and press your palms on the table, spreading your fingers. "I'm still proving myself. If you think you have anything to prove to me, it's only that you're forgiving, and you've already done that several times. You're here with me, and that's more than I deserve from you."

We hold each other's eyes for a long moment, making sure we're okay. Are we okay? I don't know.

"Do you feel better about us now?" You reach across and take my hand again. "Never think you need to prove anything to me, Rachael. It'll always be me who needs to prove I'm worthy of you." You lean forward and kiss my knuckles, then spread my hand and kiss my palm. "You're an incredible woman, and you don't even realize it. Smart, beautiful, and always a contradiction. Sometimes timid, sometimes outrageously sexy. Sometimes insecure and other times assertive and confident. I never know who you'll be next, but your heart is constant, giving, kind, caring, loyal. You amaze me daily, Rachael."

My constant, giving, kind, caring and loyal heart somersaults. You're not the same man you were on the island. You're more forthcoming, more on edge. This has to be the Merrick Rocha who dashes in to acquire property he might not be able to have. Everything's on the line, and you're not a man who gives up on what you want.

"What happens when I stop amazing you? I'm not here for your amusement or idolatry."

Your lips quirk, but you do your best not to smile. "You're always amusing to me. And I do idolize you. I aspire to be more like you, to have your heart, to have your soul. You can teach me and give me what I'm missing."

I swallow hard past a lump forming in my throat. "That's a lot to ask of me. What if I can't?"

"What if *I* can't? What if I fail you? You only have to be yourself. I'm the one who has to change." You kiss my knuckles again and lean your forehead against them. "What if you don't want me? What if I can't stop hurting you, and I don't even realize I'm doing it?"

You're afraid, too. It's calming to see your confidence crack. I'm not the only with without all the answers. I run my fingers through your hair, loving the feeling of the silky waves tickling my fingers. "I guess we'll have to muddle through together, won't we?"

You raise your head, clenching your jaw, your eyes shiny. You blink a few times, and I realize you have tears in your eyes. "Please. Please, let's get through this," you whisper. "I need you. You're real. You don't care about my money or my company. You see *me*, not the Merrick Rocha everyone else sees."

Reaching up, I stroke your cheek and run my thumb over your lips. "You have so many different Merrick's inside of you. There's the strong and confident, insanely sensual man, but at times like this, you're a hurt little boy. It doesn't take a degree in psychology to see why you push people away. You can't stand to think of them leaving you, rejecting you on their own terms, so you give them a reason. I won't let you push me away anymore, even if it's unintentional."

You squeeze my hand so hard, it hurts. Your eyes dart back and forth in desperation. "Tell me when I'm hurting your feelings. Don't leave me again. Promise me."

I step off the cliff and plunge into unknown depths. "I promise. I won't leave you again."

You close your eyes, your chest deflates and shoulders relax. When you open them, you gaze at me with such intense emotion; it washes over me and makes me inhale sharply. "Can we get out of here now?" you ask. "I need to hold you."

I push my chair out and you follow my lead. We head outside hand-in-hand. At the S.U.V., you open my door.

Before getting in, I put a hand on your cheek. "We've started over, so you can touch me now." I rise up on my toes and kiss you, hard.

You groan and squeeze my hip. "I can't believe I'm saying this, but I just want to hold you for now. I just want to be close to you and know you're with me." You lean down and kiss me, barely brushing your lips against mine. "If I kiss you deeper, I might not be able to control myself." Your nose nuzzles mine. "Is that okay with you?"

I kiss you again. "I'm going to need to kiss these lips. I'm addicted. You're going to have to find a way to control yourself." I step back and shrug. "If that's what you really want."

You narrow your eyes and give me a sly smile. "You're asking for trouble."

I quirk an eyebrow at you. "Maybe."

Groaning, you gesture to the S.U.V. "Get in before I take you right here on the ground."

Heat pools in my stomach and rushes lower, throbbing and eager. I run a finger down your chest, lingering at the fiy of your jeans. "Promises, promises."

You pick me up, not-so-subtly grinding into my bottom, letting me know you're hard as rock, and drop me onto the seat. "You can't go back once you give yourself to me. You know that."

"I know that."

We stare into each other's eyes for a minute before you take a deep breath and close my door. The drive back to my mom's house is silent. I wish I knew what you were thinking. It's clear you weren't expecting me to offer myself up to you. Now that I have, you're shaken. "I think you're right," I say. "We should just hold each other. For today."

Looking straight ahead, you reach over and squeeze my leg without a word.

We lay fully-clothed snuggling in my bed, the bed in my childhood bedroom, covered by a quilt my grandma made. The room's dim, the only light sneaking in under my closed shades. We're back in our secluded bubble away from the real world.

"I feel like I'm in high school and snuck in through your window." You nuzzle my ear with your nose.

"It feels like high school. Probably because my mom would have a shit fit if she knew you were here. I'll always be ten-years-old to her. It's the curse of being the only child."

Your laugh sends chills down my back. "Never had a guy in this bed then?"

"Are you kidding? She would've killed me."

You trail kisses up and down my neck. "I like that I'm the first."

"Only because you sent her away. Very sneaky, Mr. Rocha."

You shift on top of me, weaving our fingers together and resting your forehead against mine. "Strategy, Miss

DeSalvo. Strategy." Your lips press against mine, and your kiss is slow and sweet. Painfully sweet. Your tongue teases my bottom lip. Mine darts forward to meet it, but you don't accept my invitation in to explore, barely touching mine with yours. It's like a first, hesitant kiss.

"You might be taking this innocent high school routine a little too far." I pull my hands free of yours so I can thread them through your hair, press your lips tighter against mine and snake my tongue in your mouth. "Kiss me like you mean it, Merrick."

"I always mean it, Rachael."

I love hearing you say my name when you're breathless and filled with desire. "Make me feel how much you mean it."

My words break you. Your fingers curl against the sides of my face, and your mouth takes mine, owns it. I hitch my leg up over your hip and my hands find their way up the back of your shirt, caressing your warm, smooth skin. You moan into my open mouth. I tug your lip with my teeth. I don't want to hold back anymore. I grip your hand and slide it up the side of my t-shirt. "Touch me. Please. I don't want to beg you, but I will. Touch me."

"You never need to beg me, baby." Your tongue darts into my mouth, stroking against mine as your fingers tug down the cup of my bra, and your palm presses against my breast. I tear my lips from yours and throw my head back, sucking in a trembling breath. Your hand scorches like the sun after wanting your touch for so, so long.

Heated breath tickles my skin as your mouth and tongue slide down my neck. Abruptly, you sit up breaking our contact. "You made me break my rule."

I'm stunned, but your eyes are playful. "What rule? And do I get to be punished?"

Surprise flashes across your face and you laugh. "Punished? I'm not really into that scene, but if that's what you want..."

"I was only kidding, but what rule?" I slip a finger in your waistband and try to tug you back down, but you only drop your gaze to my hand without moving closer. "You have to touch me first."

"I thought we started over?"

"We can't erase what happened—what I did to you." Your eyes meet mine, filled with regret and longing. "I need you to initiate this or I'll feel like I'm taking advantage of you."

I lick my lips and slip my other hand to your zipper. "Like this?" I unbutton and unzip, pushing the denim and boxer briefs as low around your hips as I can.

Your eyes close as your cock falls forward, heavy and hard, ready for me. "Just like this, Rachael."

You ease back on your elbows, and I tug your pants down farther. "Help me. I want all of you."

You lift your hips, and I visualize myself on top of you, feeling you thrusting into me. I grab your jeans, slip them down and straddle your knees. Your hands gather in my hair as I lower my head, wrapping both hands around your thick, hard arousal.

I kiss your swollen head, finding it silky soft. I greet it with the tip of my tongue, taking it in my mouth and circling the rim. You groan, and your knees bend suddenly, tipping me forward, bringing almost your entire length into my mouth.

"Sorry," you whisper, lowering your knees. "That wasn't intentional."

I stroke you a few times, spreading the slickness from my mouth. "I liked it. I like making you lose control." Locking my eyes on yours, I lick you, starting at your base and running the flat of my tongue up to your tip before taking you back in my mouth and sucking hard.

Your dark eyes are black with desire watching me take you. "Ahh, God your mouth feels good. I haven't been in control since I met you."

I fondle your balls with one hand while stroking you with the other, my mouth sucking and slipping along your head. Your muscles quake with your effort not to thrust into me, and I know you want to be deeper.

With my hands pressing on your hips, I bob my head up and down, taking you to the back of my throat and sucking as hard as I can as I pull back. You're coming undone underneath me. Your hands come to my head and press down gently then pull back on my hair, guiding our pace. You're so big, it's hard to not scrape my teeth along your skin, but judging by the heavy panting coming from you, you like it.

Your hands cup my cheeks, and you lift my mouth off of you. Your dark eyes hooded with arousal. "I can't take anymore. It'll be over fast if you keep driving me to the edge like that." You sit up and pull my t-shirt over my head. "We don't need this." My bra goes next. "We don't need this, either."

I watch your hands cup my breasts, your thumbs stroke back and forth across my taut nipples, sending flashes of electricity between my thighs. I break you away long enough to tug your t-shirt over your head. "I'm dying to kiss you all over."

You groan. "It's my turn." Your mouth latches on to my breast, sucking and pulling. Your teeth pinch, then your tongue soothes. I arch into you, craving more. Your fingers pluck and roll my other nipple. I scoot forward and rock my hips against yours, aching for friction between my legs.

"Easy," you whisper, hot breath against my breast. "I'll get there, baby."

I lean forward and flick your earlobe with my tongue. "I *need* you to touch me."

Your mouth comes up to meet mine, searching inside, exploring and restless. "I need you to trust that I won't hurt you before we do this. Do you trust me?"

I grind into you again. "I'm more than ready for you. You won't hurt me."

You hold my hips firm so I can't move. "I don't mean physically. I want you to give yourself to me completely. Not just your body." You brush my hair back from my forehead, gazing into my eyes desperate to find the answer you're longing for. "Do you trust me with your heart?"

My body starts to tremble. How can I possibly trust you with my heart? You've torn me apart and you don't know how to stop yourself from doing it again. "I thought this was about sex. That we were getting past this one barrier. Now you're asking me for my heart?"

You brush my cheek with your fingertips before laying me on my back and shifting your body down beside mine. "How many men have you been with, Rachael?"

"What does that have to do with anything? How many women have you been with?"

You grin. "I won't avoid that question, but I'm guessing you haven't been with many. You're not the type of woman to give your body without love. Am I wrong?"

My eyes flicker to yours, then the ceiling. "No."

You grasp my chin and turn my head, making me look at you. Your eyes are heated and intense. I can't look away even if I wanted to. "Then you either love me, or you're willing to sacrifice your standards for me. Which is it?"

"I don't know. I'm trying not to think about it." Something lodges in my throat. It might be my heart. Tears spring to my eyes, and I desperately blink them back.

You press my head against your chest. "I won't let you sacrifice anything to be with me. I'm not worth it, Rachael. If by some miracle, I can earn your trust then we'll do this. Now's not the time though."

"It's my body to do with what I want." I'm still burning for you, and I'm so ashamed that you stopped me and called me out on my intentions.

"Not when you're doing it with mine. I don't want you to regret us." You bring my hand to your lips. "I have a lot to make up for. I'm trying to be careful." You tilt my chin up. "I don't have anything with me anyway. I'm guessing you don't keep a box of condoms here for emergencies." A flirtatious glint sparks in your eyes as you chuckle.

"Not exactly, no." I squirm in discomfort, still throbbing and aching for release. Guess I'll be giving that to myself in the bathroom. "I'll be back."

I try to sit up, but you grab my arm and push me back on the pillows. "I'm not done with you yet." Your hands run down over my breasts, followed by your lips. "I didn't mean you wouldn't have your turn." Your eyes look up at me while your tongue circles my belly button. "I won't be inside you until you trust me, but I won't leave you like this, Rachael."

My jeans are undone, shoved down and pulled off in what seems like two seconds. Your nose nuzzles along the lacy waistband of my underwear. Dark waves of your hair tickle my stomach. Squeezing my calves, your hands slide up my legs and push my thighs far, far apart. You run your nose farther down, stopping over my sensitive bundle of nerves, and inhale deeply. "You smell so good. Wet and ready for me." You nuzzle your nose and make me writhe before planting a soft kiss over my opening.

You slip a finger under the elastic on one side of my

panties and tug it aside revealing me. You let out a low, breathy groan and dip your finger between my slick lips. "So wet."

I squeeze the quilt in my fists and watch you kiss my small patch of curls as you slide your finger inside me. "Ah...God." I thrust against your finger, needing more.

You tug my panties off before your mouth closes over my clit and you push two fingers inside me. "You're so tight and hot." Your breath whispers across my sensitive nerves making me gasp and grab your hair. One of your hands leaves my thigh to cup my butt and lift me up, rocking me against your fingers and mouth.

I hold your head tight between my legs. I'm on fire and only your tongue can give me relief. The way you alternate between sucking and licking—fast and hard, soft and long—and slowly moving your fingers in and out against my front wall, makes me want to scream. You're driving me mad. The ball of tension waiting to explode inside me gets bigger and bigger by the second. "I'm going to come so hard." My voice isn't mine. It's brash and wanton. There's a sex goddess in the room with us. It can't be me. I'd never say something like that.

You moan, sending vibrations through your lips. I buck, my back arches off the bed. "God, Merrick."

I can't think. My body is nothing but sensation and greedy lust, striving and pulsing for release.

"Your almost there, baby. God, your gripping my fingers so fucking tight."

You set me back down on the bed and stroke yourself. The sight makes my mouth water. "Let me." I reach for you, grabbing your shoulders and pulling. "I want you back in my mouth."

You turn around and position us in a sideways sixty-nine. "I hope you're okay with this, because you taste like heaven, and I'm not taking my tongue away until you come."

Before I can answer, you dive back between my legs, devouring, pushing your tongue inside me. The cries and moans filling the room can't be from me. I've never made sounds like this during sex. "God, it feels so good," I whimper, taking you in both hands.

I run my lips down your shaft, darting my tongue out to taste you. Your lips and tongue mirror mine. "Show me what you like," you say.

"Everything. I love it all."

"How about this?" You slide your tongue down my middle, circle my opening and keep going, back to my anus.

I clench and jolt forward into your chin. "I don't...I've never..."

You reach down and fold your hand over mine, loosening my death grip on your shaft. "Relax, baby. We'll save that for another time." You kiss your way back to my front, pressing my thighs open. "There's so much I want to do to you."

Right now there's one thing I'm dying to do to you. I suck you deep into my mouth trying to take your entire length, but failing. You're too big and hit the back of my throat. I pull back and delve down again, sucking and flicking my tongue.

"Shit." Your release a hiss of air through your teeth and pull me in tighter against your mouth, relentlessly sucking my clit.

Heat expands like an inferno inside me, urging my body to thrust and rock against you. I grab your hips and take you in and out of my mouth at the same pace. I moan and suck you harder and faster as my orgasm builds and builds.

"Oh god. Oh god, Merrick, I'm coming." I explode, cry out and throw my head back, locking my thighs around your face as my insides throb and grip. You draw it out with your fingers pumping in and out of me.

"Yes, Rachael. You're perfect." I open my legs and come back to my senses to find you stroking yourself.

I lick your head as you pump. "Give it to me. Come in my mouth."

"Fuck, Rach!" You shudder and stroke hard twice before erupting on my tongue. I swallow all you give me and lick my lips.

You roll to your back. "Jesus. I think I died. Twice. And I haven't even been inside you yet." You grab my foot and kiss my big toe.

"That was better than any sex I've ever had. I can't imagine…"

"I know." You sit up and turn around, lying beside me

on my pillow. The look in your eyes can only be described as wonder. Your finger trails over my chin, down my neck and between my breasts. "I've never been so in sync with someone in my life." You kiss me, soft and slow, smelling and tasting of my pleasure. "Physically as well as mentally." Your lips press against my forehead. "I've always wanted to find you."

I snuggle into your warm chest, trying to ignore the finger jabs in my brain telling me to slow down. Last time we were together, you wanted a threesome with Joan. How has that changed? Has it?

"What are you thinking?" you ask, twining your fingers through my hair.

"About Joan."

Your fingers still. "What about her?"

"You're obviously pretty close to her, comfortable with her. She's more than your assistant."

You lift my chin and kiss me deeply. "Don't." Your dark eyes search mine, pleading. "She doesn't mean anything to me. What we had was physical. It began abruptly and ended after it was out of our systems. Because I trust her and have been with her in the past, I thought she could help us. I was stupid—as usual. Please don't hold it against me."

"How can I not think about it, though, every time you're together? You didn't hesitate being with her again."

"*With you*, Rachael. Only with you. I would've never been alone with her. It's not her I want." Your arms tighten around my waist, pulling the length of our bodies as close as you can get them. Your cheek presses against mine, your lips scour my neck with kisses. "Believe me."

I need time to think. My head, heart and body jumped at the chance to start over with you. Now I'm back-pedaling. I want you, and I can forgive you, but I can't forget. I keep stumbling over memories, over the hurt you've inflicted in the short time we've known each other. How much more is to come? How much more can I take and push to the back of my mind?

"I barely know you," I whisper. And it's the truth. We've been led by our bodies, our unrequited desire. Inside our bubble on Turtle Tear it was real. Outside the bubble, I'm not so sure.

"You know me better than anyone else does." You brush the hair off my forehead and stroke my cheek with your thumb. "You see past the money to me, the fucked up man inside. I try to keep him hidden, but I can't hide from you. I don't want to hide from you; I want to be better for you."

"There's nothing fucked up about you." I twist my finger through a wave of hair falling over your brow. "You have a communication problem, that's all."

"You don't think I'm controlling?"

I twist and tap my lips. "You? Controlling?" I laugh. "You couldn't control me if you tried, Merrick. My mother already does."

You roll onto your back with a sigh and rest your arm over your head. "Exactly. She's the reason I'm in this damn mess. If you would've just come to work for me, I wouldn't have acted like such a jackass." Your eyes crinkle with the quirk of your lips. "I blame her. You should to. Then you'd trust me, and we can get on with things."

"Things?" I grin and shrug my eyebrows suggestively.

"Things." You run a hand between my legs. I sigh and close my eyes, rubbing against your fingers. "Later, baby." You take your hand away and kiss me, soft and slow. "We have all the time in the world if you want it."

"I want it...now. I can't have you laying here beside me naked and denying me. If you don't want to, then we need to get dressed."

"Oh no!" You laugh and tug me on top of you, tickling me. "You're not going to say I don't want to. You know that's a lie."

I laugh so hard with your fingers digging into my sides, I can barely breathe. "Stop!" I try to push you way, but your arms come around me and hold me tight.

"Just think how good it'll be when you trust me, Rachael. When it's the right time. Thinking about it..." You roll your eyes and groan. "It's hard, but I can be patient. When you're ready to give yourself to me completely, it'll be better than anything."

Hearing the sincerity in your voice, and seeing your face, so serious and intense, I feel like a gift you're waiting to unwrap. I trail a finger down the side of your face and brush my lips against yours. You're a gift. I know you are. A gift forced upon me at first, but now that I've had a peek at what's inside the box, I know you're a gift I never want to give up.

"I can't believe I'm lying naked in the bed you slept in as a little girl." You wrap the ends of the quilt around us. "It's not somewhere I ever imagined being with you like this."

"It's nice." I run my lips down the bridge of your nose. "I always wanted a guy in this bed with me."

"I bet you were a horny little teenage chick, weren't you?" You poke my side, making me squirm.

"You have no idea."

Your eyebrows shoot up and your dimples blossom in your cheeks. "Girls Gone Wild?"

A spurt of laughter erupts from my throat. "Hardly. I was shy. I had one boyfriend for six months of my senior year."

"He was the lucky one, huh?"

I thread my fingers through your hair, loving how the silky smooth locks feel running between them. "I wouldn't say lucky, but he was the first."

You raise you head and nip my neck. "He was one lucky bastard."

"What about you? Tell me about your first time."

Your eyes follow your finger across my collarbone and your expression sobers. "It wasn't altogether memorable."

"You have to remember your first time."

You grimace, but only for a second. "It's hazy."

"Were you drunk?" There's a story you're hiding from me. You said you didn't want to hide.

"No. It's more like selective memory. I selected not to remember it." You squeeze me and kiss my shoulder.

"Why? Was it bad?"

You nuzzle into my neck. You won't look at me. "I was young. Too young."

"How young?"

"Twelve."

I shove your shoulders down so you have to look at me. "Twelve? Merrick! How?"

You smirk. "I think you know how, Rachael."

I purse my lips. I don't need sarcasm right now. "With who? Did you want to?"

You laugh. "Hell yes I wanted to. I shouldn't have, but I wanted to. She was fifteen. The babysitter. Heidi was asleep. Dad wasn't home."

"Wow," I whisper. "The babysitter. Did she initiate it or did you?"

A crease forms between your brows. "I'm not sure. It just kind of happened. It was fast." You chuckle. "I'm sure you can imagine my prowess at twelve. Two Pump Pete."

"Did you use protection?"

You drop your eyes and shake your head. "I had no idea what I was getting into."

"You were too young. She didn't..."

The words *get pregnant* linger unspoken between us.

Your eyes close. You're barely breathing. "Her parents paid a visit to my dad. They said they'd take care of it. I never found out *how* they took care of it."

I bolt upright, straddling you, slapping my hands over my mouth. "Oh my God, Merrick. You could have a kid out there somewhere."

You shake your head, your eyes wide with panic, and grab my thighs. "No way. It's not like I'm hard to find. She would've had me in court paying back child support by now. She would've taken me for millions if she had my kid."

"Have you tried to find her? How can you not know? Doesn't it drive you crazy?"

The corners of your lips tug down, and you turn your eyes from mine. "I don't know her last name." You pat my leg. "My first and probably biggest fuck up."

I grab your chin and make you look at me. "Your dad probably knows her last name and what happened. You need to ask him."

You hold my wrist and ease my hand from your face. "I won't speak to him for any reason."

I curl my arms around your hand and hold it against my chest. "He—or she—would be about twenty now. Someone to take over your business since you're so hell-bent on hiding out at the hotel and dropping out of your current life."

Your chest expands and your face tightens into a pained expression. "Don't," you whisper. "Please. I can't think there's anyone out there."

I lean back down, my chest against yours, and slide my hands under your neck. "What are you so afraid of?"

"I'm not a good man, Rachael." Your voice cracks. "I can't be someone's father. I'd be no better than my own."

I sit back up and poke my finger into your chest. "That. Is. A. Lie. You know you wouldn't be like him. He abused you. You wouldn't do that."

You pick my hand up and squeeze my finger. "I wouldn't call it abuse. That would mean he didn't ignore me entirely."

"Neglect is abuse. He neglected you, didn't he?"

You shrug. "He got me a babysitter."

We both burst out laughing even though it's not something to find funny. At least it relieves the wave of sadness that had washed over us.

"Fine. I'll let it go. For now." I trace my fingertip over your lips then lean down and kiss you, first your upper lip, then your lower, teasing and tender. "I'm glad you told me. This is how you get me to trust you, by opening up to me."

"I'm an open book for you, Rachael. Ask me anything."

I'm addicted to your lips. "I would if I could stop kissing you long enough."

"Ask me later." You grab me in a bear hug and roll me back over with your lips pressed to mine, both of us laughing.

This is real. We're not in Turtle Tear, but it's real—a new real, somewhere to start at least. And I like how we're starting.

"This is new," I say, taking a bite of my burger. We're sitting at an outside table under an umbrella at a small restaurant downtown.

You swallow a sip of your Coke. "What's new?"

"Us eating together." I wink.

You grin. "Only because we're in public." You reach under the table and pull my foot up onto your lap, nestling it right between your legs. "But we can be discrete."

I tap my foot against you lightly. "You must trust me to be in this position." I pop a fry into my mouth and giggle.

You make a throaty, growling sound. "I trust that you want me to be able to use it sometime in the near future."

The waiter stops at our table and glances back and forth between us. He knows he's interrupted something very personal by the embarrassed look on his face. "Can I get you anything else?"

You grind my foot against you. "I think we have all we need."

I pull my lips in, smothering a laugh as the waiter leaves the bill on the table. When he leaves, I tug my foot away from you. "Will you ever let me have a meal in peace?"

"Probably not." You pick up a cherry tomato from your salad and hold it up to my lips. When I open my mouth, you pop it in and I kiss your fingers. "You're too tantalizing to resist when your mouth is full and your lips are moving. Reminds me of how you looked this morning when your mouth was full of me."

"Shh!" I almost choke and dart my eyes around us to see if anyone has heard you while you crack up laughing. "It's not funny."

"The look on your face is priceless."

I can't help it, your laugh is contagious and soon we're both sitting there snickering. I stand up and stick a finger in your dimple. "Are you ready to go, or do you want to humiliate me some more?"

You throw some cash on the table and take my hand. "Where are we going?"

"I don't know. Back to my mom's I guess."

"Why not your apartment? Are you avoiding more humiliation?"

I turn to you, uncertain what you mean. "What are you talking about?"

"Are you embarrassed to introduce me to Shannon? Would it be awkward for you?"

"Awkward? No. She's just..." I cringe. "Nosey. Pushy. Opinionated. She'll ask personal questions and make innuendos. Then she'll never leave me alone about what I should do with you and when and how. She's the one who will embarrass me, not you."

You tilt your head and narrow your eyes. "Are you attracted to people who want to control you, or do they seek you out?"

I put my hands on my hips and glower at you. "Well, in your case, you sought me out."

You laugh and take my hand again, leading me down the sidewalk. "I thought you said you didn't find me controlling."

"Only because that position is taken in my life, but you want to. You control everything in your world."

"Does that mean I can count on you to be *in my world*?" You swing our hands between us.

"Yes. I thought we got past this."

"Then you're going back with me?"

I stop walking. The thought of going back there—with Joan—sends a shock of panic through me. "I don't know."

"Why is your hand shaking? What's wrong?" You pull me into a hug and hold me. "Tell me why you're upset all the sudden."

"I can still feel her touching me," I whisper.

You sigh and press your forehead against mine, holding my head in your hands. "I'm so sorry, Rachael. I didn't know you'd react this way. I never would've—"

"Stop." I press my hands against your chest. "I let her do it. I'm just not sure how to wrap my head around that fact."

You jerk back to look at me. "What do you mean? What's to wrap your head around?"

I throw my hands up. "Merrick. I let another woman... *fondle* me."

You shake your head not following my dilemma. "Yeah..."

I watch my foot slide in and out of my sandal, clasp and unclasp my hands. "I didn't stop her right away."

Your hands rest on my shoulders. When I glance up, one side of your mouth quirks. "Because you liked it. It's okay that you liked it."

"Is it?" My heart pounds. "I've never thought about a woman touching me."

You caress my cheek. "Rach, it doesn't mean you want women now. If she would've wandered into the bedroom and you were alone, would you have let her touch you?"

"No. It was what you wanted. I did it for you."

"You liked it because it was me touching you through her. It was for us. I wanted you to like it." You cup my face with both hands and kiss me. "We'll never do it again. Only I can touch you. Okay?"

I stare into your deep, dark eyes and smile. "Only you can touch me, huh? You really are a control freak." I grab the back of your head and pull you in for another kiss. "It's a deal."

Your hand whacks my backside with a sharp crack. "I didn't forget you asked me to punish you."

I pinch your nipples through your t-shirt and twist. "I'll punish you back."

"Ow!" You pull my hands away, laughing. "Woman, you're going to be the death of me."

Fifteen

Standing hand-in-hand on my mom's front porch, you lean down and place a soft kiss under my ear. "I have some work to do before a meeting with my lawyer. I'd like you to come along tonight so I can introduce you. We're settling some paperwork and having drinks in the bar at the hotel."

I kiss you under your chin. "Where are you staying?"

"The Ritz Carlton. Can you make it? Nine o'clock?" Your lips trail along my jaw.

I'm addicted to your touch, your kiss, the feel of your warm body under my hands and lips, your smell, your voice. "I'll be there."

Your mouth claims mine in a slow, deep kiss that feels like you're weaving a spell with your tongue, putting me in a trance. I never want it to end.

After I watch you drive away, I pull out my cell and call Shannon. "Help!" I say when she answers. "I'm meeting Merrick's lawyer tonight and have no idea what to wear."

"God, I thought you had an accident or something! Never say 'help' as soon as I answer again unless you're seconds from death."

"Sorry." I bite my cheek so I don't laugh. "Where are you? Want to go to the mall?"

"Of course I want to go to the mall. I'll be by in a few to pick you up."

"I can drive." I sit back on the porch swing and rock.

"Rach, you know I hate your driving. Be there soon."

Flipping through racks of silky, sleeveless blouses, Shannon pulls a light blue one out and holds it up to me. "Is tonight casual? I'm at a loss. We could go with this blouse and a black skirt, or is that overdoing it?"

"No clue. That's why I called you." I fiddle with the tag attached to the seam, turning it to look at the price. "A hundred and forty-five bucks. This one's staying home on the rack tonight."

Shannon rolls her eyes. "Can't you charge it? The color's perfect with your tan."

"No." I pull the hanger from her fingers and shove it back on the rack.

"I know," Shannon says, her eyes landing on a manne-quin behind me. "Sundress. Dark colors so you don't look like you're going to a picnic, but not formal either. Fun and flirty, but still somewhat dressy."

She pulls five from a nearby rounder and pushes me toward the fitting rooms. "Try these on."

Ten minutes later, I have my choice narrowed down to the one dress that actually fits me and doesn't look like a sack. It's ankle-length with black, white and navy blue designs, thin straps and a gathered bust twisted in the center.

"Perfect," Shannon says when I model for her. "You look like you have boobs." Her phone's to her ear, and she holds up one finger to me. "It *is* an emergency," she says to whoever she's talking to. "Yes, five-fifteen works. Thank you so much!" She hangs up and tosses her phone in her bag. "You're getting highlights at five-fifteen. Let's find some strappy, fuck-me- pumps to wear with that dress."

She spins and saunters off, all golden blonde with sunshine streaks. I have to admit, she always has nice hair. "I'm aiming for heels I can walk in and not fall on my ass."

Shannon turns with a cocked eyebrow. "Honey, I've seen Merrick. You get your claws into a man like him and hang on for dear life. You're leaving here with every advantage modern retail can give you. Got it?"

Following her to the shoe department, I can't help but smile thinking about what she'd say if she knew I'd been wearing your oversized t-shirts and basketball shorts for the past week, hair in a ponytail and no makeup.

But maybe she's right. You and I have started over. The playing field has changed. We're back in civilization. What if you realize I'm not sophisticated, that I don't fit into your high-class business world, your billionaire social circles?

I'm being paranoid. You watched me for three months. You know the real me.

Shannon makes a beeline for a pair of platform silver sandals with crisscrossing straps up the ankles. *"These."* She flags down a sales associate and pushes my shoulder into a chair.

"I thought we were going for sexy, not hooker." I turn around and pick up a black pair. "I like these. They're strappy sandals like those, but without the platform and sky-high heels."

Shannon sighs. "Rach."

I sigh back. "Shannon. I seriously don't want to end up with this dress over my head in the middle of the Ritz bar because of those shoes."

"I'm trying to get your dress over your head in Merrick's bed because of *these* shoes." She points to the silver heel in her hand. "Trust me?"

Her determination makes me smile. "Fine. But I don't need shoes to get me there." I need to trust you and prove to you that I do.

Shannon narrows her eyes and a sly smile slides across her lips. "So, have you then?"

I glance to the sales lady walking toward us, playing her question off. "Maybe. Maybe not."

"You bitch!" She smacks my arm. The sales lady stops, not sure if we're fighting for real. When Shannon starts laughing, she approaches. "We need this in an eight," Shannon says, not waiting for the woman to ask how she can help us.

She plops down in the chair beside me to wait for the sales lady to come back with the hooker shoes, and stares holes in the side of my face until I look at her. "Everything but," I tell her, feeling my face flush. "Pretty much."

She lifts her hands from the arms of the chair and smacks them back down, gripping them tight. "When? And why didn't you tell me? And why the "but"?"

"This morning. I am telling you, and the "but" is because it's just not the right time yet."

Her eyes widen in disbelief. *"It's not the right—Rach!* What are you waiting for? A ring?"

"No! We both want to wait until it's the right time. That's all. No big deal." I scoot forward and slip my shoes off, seeing the sales lady returning.

"Here we are," she says, handing me the box. "Do you need help trying these on?"

"No, I've got it. Thanks." I take the lid off and pull a shoe out. "Wow, these are...something."

"Just put it on." Shannon shifts in her chair to get a better view.

I buckle the straps and stand, holding my hands out for balance. "I don't know."

She bolts to her feet clapping. "They're perfect! Put them in the box! We need to get your hair done."

Humoring her, I buy the shoes and hope for the best. "If I embarrass myself, I'm blaming you."

"Fine," she says, slinging an arm around my shoulder. "You can blame me for landing you an incredible piece of man ass, too."

At nine o'clock, I enter the Ritz Carlton lobby, surprisingly stable on top of the high heels clicking on the marble floor. My hair is amazing, caramel and gold highlights nestled against my natural dark brown. I'll never let anyone else touch it.

Shannon knows what she's doing in the hair and makeup department. She applied smoky eye shadow on my lids, bronzer on my cheeks and a pinkish-brown gloss on my lips—to accentuate my tan she said.

I'm hot. I can't keep the smile off my face, and I've never felt more confident. Excitement and anticipation bubble through me. I'm like a bottle of champagne ready to burst.

"Rachael!" you call, striding toward me. Your face lights up as you get closer. "Jesus, you look good enough to eat." You pull me against your chest and whisper in my ear, "We might have to skip this meeting and go to my room so I can do just that." You nuzzle your nose in my hair and nip my earlobe.

Heat flushes my chest. "You look pretty tasty yourself." I run my hands up and down your long, lean, muscled back over your black dress shirt rolled up to your elbows. Your tan slacks hang perfectly on your hips making my fingers itch to unbuckle your belt. "I hope this isn't a long meeting."

"We've almost wrapped up. Only one more paper to sign."

You take my hand and kiss it before leading me to the lounge off the sixth floor lobby. I've never been in the Ritz Carlton hotel before and the lounge is nothing like any bar I've ever been in. The large room with plush blue chairs at circular tables, sofas, a marble fireplace and a small bar at one end is more like a stuffy relative's living room than a bar. Drinking tea and eating scones would be more appropriate than sipping alcohol.

I glance down at my strappy, silver, platform sandals that are more nightclub than Windsor Castle and feel entirely out of place.

There aren't more than fifteen other people sitting in small groups of two or three around the room. At a table in the corner, an older man in a gray suit sits alone making notes with a gold pen. He sees us approach, stands and extends his hand. "Ms. DeSalvo. It's a pleasure to make your acquaintance." He takes my hand and smiles with bright, yet coffee-stained teeth.

"Please, call me Rachael."

"This is my lawyer," you say, "Maxwell Campbell."

"Call me Max," he says as you pull out my chair.

"What can I get you to drink?" you ask. "Wine or something stronger tonight?" A dimple winks in your cheek.

"They have an extensive martini list," Max says, crossing his legs and adjusting his suit jacket. "Rocktails they call them. Named after rock songs."

"Surprise me." I'm too nervous about being here, in your element, with your lawyer to deliberate a drink choice.

"I'm full of surprises." You wink and turn toward the bar.

Max stares at me with his head slightly cocked, like he's trying to figure me out. "Well," he says, pulling his eyes away and picking up a pair of glasses on the table. "Merrick certainly is full of surprises, I'll give him that."

Is he referring to me? I guess a woman like me would be a surprise for you to have on your arm. "Yes, he is."

I watch your back. The last time it was faced toward me and you were standing at a bar, I ended up unconscious for two days. Not that I have any fear of that happening again. My eyes are on you willing you to hurry back to me.

"How did you find Turtle Tear, Rachael? Was it what you thought it would be?" Max peers over top of his frames with piercing glass-blue eyes. His tone's not unfriendly, but something in his demeanor has me on edge.

"I love Turtle Tear. It's more than I ever imagined it to be."

"Here you go," you say, putting a hand on my shoulder and sitting a martini glass in front of me with a curved, blue, blown-glass stem. It's shaped like a crescent moon. "It's a Champagne Supernova."

"Thank you. It sounds great."

You trail a finger across the back of my neck as you walk behind my chair and settle into yours. "I have something to tell you." You take my hand firmly in both of yours. Your dark eyes claim mine, and a ghost of a smile crosses your lips. "The only signature Max and I need is yours. I'm giving you Turtle Tear. It's yours."

I inhale and hold my breath. This can't be happening. My head spins. I grab the table with my free hand. "You can't. I can't accept that."

Your smile widens. "Remember when I told you it was yours. I wasn't kidding." Your eyes flicker to Max and back to me before saying, "I *had* to get you there, Rachael. This is why. I knew the hotel and the island belonged to you the first time we spoke."

"All we need is a signature," Max says, handing me his gold pen with a strangled smile and sliding a piece of paper across the table. "Beside the "X"."

I lean toward you and whisper. "Can we talk about this, please?"

You brush a strand of hair back behind my shoulder. "Of course. After you sign."

"Merrick—"

You place a finger over my lips. "I'm not asking, Rachael. It's yours. That document is the title to the property. I've already signed it over."

"Why? I don't...I'm nothing to you."

Your chin drops, and your eyes go wide. "How can you think that? You have to know that's not true."

I shake my head. "I didn't mean...I'm not a relative or anything. Why not give it to Heidi or one of her kids if you don't want to keep it?"

You let my hand go and smack your palm lightly on the table as you sit back in your chair. "No. It's yours. Please sign the title."

You gaze across the room. This conversation is closed. Fine. I'll sign and then give the hotel to Heidi myself. I pick up the pen and whisk my name across the line in black ink.

"Congratulations," Max says, snapping up the title and closing it in a file inside his briefcase. He picks up a rocks glass on the table with a lime floating in clear liquid and ice. "To a successful renovation."

I lift my glass and turn my eyes to you. Your chest fills as you smile in relief and lift your rocks glass. The three of us toast, and your hand cups my knee under the table. "Thank you," I say. "I can't begin to understand…"

You lean over and press a kiss on my cheek. "I'm not asking you to understand. I only hope you won't kick me off the island." You chuckle and kiss me again, quickly on the lips this time.

"Why would I ever do that?" I tease, and lift my mouth to yours for a longer kiss this time.

"Well," Max says.

You and I part, reluctantly. Max stands and lifts his briefcase. "I'll leave you two to celebrate." We both stand, and he shakes your hand then mine. "Congratulations again, Rachael. Please let me know if you ever need anything."

"Thank you. It was nice meeting you."

"Likewise."

We watch him exit the lounge, and you pull me against you. "Thank God, I have you to myself." You tap my martini glass with a finger. "Please tell me you don't want this, and we can go to my room. Hell," you lift me off my feet, "I'll get fifty of them sent to the room if you do want it. I'm taking you. Now."

I hope your meaning of *taking me* doesn't just mean to your room, because I need you inside me so badly I could die.

Sixteen

We sit on opposite sides of the jetted tub. My feet are in your lap, and your thumbs dig into my arches. Bubbles tickle my skin. You're completely relaxed with your eyes closed and your head leaning back against the edge. "You better not fall asleep on me," I warn.

"Never," you say, a slow, sexy smile crawling across your lips.

"Why, Merrick? I don't understand." There's something behind your eyes, something hidden. I don't want anything in our way. I can't take a new challenge to get past if I want you.

"Why not, Rachael?" You sit forward, running your hand up my calf, over my knee, gliding between my thighs.

"You're too good at distraction." I moan, rocking against your hand. My foot finds you hard and thick, and I guide my arch up and down your length, stroking over and over. "You have to tell me. I know there's a reason you're not telling me."

"Is this a good distraction?" You slip a finger inside me and follow it with a second. Your other hand clasps my breast. Your fingers pinch and pluck my nipple.

"Oh..." I roll my hips and arch my back. "God."

"What were you saying?" You chuckle and circle your thumb over my clit as your fingers move inside me.

"I was—oh!" Your fingers spark flames through me. My muscles contract and spasm. I explode in a rush of heat and melt in the bubbling water.

You pull me onto your lap and press your mouth to mine. Your kiss is tender and leaves me breathless. You lean your head against mine and caress my cheek. "You're so sweet when you do that. I could watch you over and over."

"I want you so much. You have to tell me why you gave me the hotel." Your chest is slick under my hands. I run them up your neck and tangle my fingers in your hair. "I want to trust you. You have to let me. No secrets."

You kiss me again, taking my bottom lip in your mouth before letting go. "I'll tell you. Let's get out first."

After stepping over the side, you scoop me out of the water and lay me in the center of the bed. "You sure we can't talk later?" The lust in your eyes is unmistakable as they run over my body, and you lick your lips.

You straddle my legs and hold yourself over me dripping water onto my chest and neck. "You talk. I can't wait." I lift my mouth to your shoulder and lick droplets off your hot, wet skin.

You groan and push your knee between mine to open me to you.

"No." I sit up and scoot back. "You talk. I play. You don't talk, we don't play."

You let out a huge sigh and shake your head, smiling. "Of all the women I could've kidnapped."

I get to my knees and press your shoulders, leading you

down onto your back. "Hands above your head and keep them there. You took me, now I get to torture you."

Sitting on your stomach with your long, hard arousal wedged snuggly between my ass cheeks, I run a fingernail down your chest, over your nipple. "Talk."

"When my grandpa died," you suck air through your teeth as I lick the nipple I scratched, "Heidi and I got the properties, but we weren't old enough to own them, to own Rocha Enterprises. My dad didn't sell me the business until I'd already become very, very wealthy. Since he owned it in name when it went international, he wants it all. He can have it all, but not Turtle Tear."

I sit up and still your hips pressing into me. "That's why you did it. To keep the hotel out of his hands. That's why you took me."

You clasp my wrists. "That's why. I'd been looking for someone who appreciated it as much as I do. When you came along—"

I shut you up by thrusting my tongue in your mouth. I know what you did when I came along. Now I understand your desperation. If anyone would try to take Turtle Tear from me, I'd do whatever I had to keep it.

You push me to my back and break the kiss. "He'd tear it down. I couldn't let him do that." Your eyes are black granite.

"It's safe now. You trusted me with it. You know I'll cherish it."

You press your palm into my thigh and drag it up over

my hip and my stomach stopping on top of my heart. You lift your hand and kiss where my pulse is pounding. "If you trust me with this, you know *I'll* cherish it."

I hold your face between my hands. "Like I've ever had a choice." I kiss your forehead, both of your cheeks, your chin. "You stormed into my life and took it over. I didn't have to give in, but God, you're impossible to resist."

Your mouth overtakes mine in a relentless, possessive kiss that leaves no question whether this is it or not. This is it. Finally. "I trust you, Merrick," I whisper, breathless and panting. "Please. No stopping." I reach between your thighs and grip you, stroke you. "I want you inside me."

"I will be. Let me touch you, taste you more first." You take my breast in your mouth, sucking and teasing the nipple with your tongue while your hand slides between my thighs. I let them fall apart and your fingers glide through my slick folds. You alternate between sweet little circles on my clit that send sparks through my core and have me writhing, to slipping those talented fingers inside me, pressing and rubbing in just the right spot to make me thrust and rock into your hand.

"Oh God, I'm going to—"

"No," you whisper, your breath hot against my wet nipple, "don't come until I'm inside you, Rachael."

Your fingers pull out of me. You kneel between my thighs and roll on a condom. "I've never needed a woman this much. I never will." The head of your cock nestles against my opening and you lean over me, resting on your forearms. Your eyes lock with mine and you thrust into me—hard.

"Ahh, you're so big!" I'm stretched and your thickness fills me, rubs all the right spots. "If you move I'll come—oh God, please." I grab your perfect ass and arch into you, thrusting and rocking my hips. "Yeah, right there!"

You're not moving, just staying deep, deep inside me and letting me fuck you to make myself come. You kiss, lick and nip my neck and lift my butt up off the bed. The angle intensifies the slow, smolder building to an explosion inside me. "That's right, baby. Take it. Take everything from me. Everything you need. Everything you want."

"Yes, I'm so close." I wrap my legs around yours and grind my hips into you. "So close," I whimper.

Slowly, you pull out, only inches, and thrust back in. Devastatingly slow. It feels so perfect, my eyes water. "Let go." You kiss my forehead. "I've got you. Take it."

Your hips roll, and fire ignites inside me. I throw my arms out to the side, gripping the sheets. "*Yesyesyesyes.* God, Merrick." I moan and gasp. You lift yourself to your knees, still thrusting, and rub my clit, intensifying the throbbing grip I have around your cock, dragging my orgasm out longer, deeper.

A sob rips through me. Nothing has ever felt this good, this satisfying. My insides are shuddering. I wanted this, and I took it. For myself. This is all mine. You're all mine.

"You're so sweet, so beautiful," you whisper. "I love giving this to you."

The rush subsides, and I take your hand away from the oversensitive bud of nerves. "That was insane."

You flip me over on top of you, driving your cock so deep inside me; I think I feel you in my stomach. I grip your thighs and lean back. "Take me again," you say. "Take all you want from me."

I lift and lower myself gently at first, then as the desire and heat begins to build again, I ride you hard, slamming down on your cock to take you deeper and harder each time, gasping and moaning with pleasure. I grip you tight inside me. I want to make you come. Want to milk every drop from you. When you groan, I know you're close. When you get even bigger, even harder inside me, I know I'm going to roll over the edge again and lose myself to you.

The familiar sensation flares and intensifies with every stroke until it explodes. I throw my head back, spineless and tingling, holding on to you so tight I can't feel my fingers. "Merrick. Ah, God. It feels so good." As soon as I come down, your thumb finds my clit, and I'm exploding again.

"Ah, fuck. Rachael. You're so tight." Your cock throbs inside me. I lean forward, pressing my palms against your abs. You squeeze my breasts as our thrusts and strokes slow and we ride out the last waves of orgasm.

I fall forward onto your chest and your arms come around me. "You're perfect." You kiss my head, stroke my hair. "You're beautiful. I don't deserve you, but I'm taking you anyway."

"That was so incredible," I mumble, surprised that I can

utter one word let alone string a few together. I try to lift myself up and groan.

"Are you okay?"

"Perfect. Give me a minute for the feeling to come back into my legs, and I'll be ready to do that all over again."

You laugh. It rumbles in your chest against my ear, mingles with the rapid beating of your heart. "I might need more than a minute. I'm definitely up for a repeat performance though. There are several more positions I'd like to put you in Miss DeSalvo."

I raise my head to find your lips. You kiss me softly, deeply. We've turned a corner. There's nothing standing between us now.

All is forgiven.

I trust you.

I've given myself to you.

Epilogue

Rachael! It's good to see you again." Beck jogs up to me and takes my suitcase. The helicopter sits on the landing pad at the airport with its propellers spinning, ready to take me home—home to Turtle Tear. "This is all you're bringing?" he gestures to the suitcase.

"The rest is being shipped at the end of the week." I reach out and hug him. I can't help it. I'm so happy to be going back and he's the first tangible part of the island that I've had contact with in weeks.

Merrick went back two weeks ago. He stayed in Cleveland until my mom got back from the cruise. He wanted to be there to meet her and help me tell her I was leaving, moving to Florida.

She refused to come with me, refused to leave her home, but she'll stay for extended visits. I promised the best room in the hotel would always be hers. She wasn't happy about me moving away, but before I left, she told me not to worry about her and that she was proud of me.

Shannon shocked me by announcing she was moving in with Seth. She said what he has between his legs is too good for him not to know what to do with it. So she's planning to teach him. Her relationships always burn bright

white, hot as the sun, then blaze out just as quickly. I hope
this one lasts.

Beck puts a hand on my head, like always, making sure
I bend down enough under the propellers. He helps me up
and in the helicopter and buckles my restraints. When he's
seated beside me and we both have our headphones on,
he turns to me and winks. "Joan works for me now, not
Merrick."

My shock has to show on my face. You didn't tell me
you'd reassigned her. "She does?"

"She does. And I plan to keep her in line and very busy,
but only with me." Beck shoots me a meaningful look.

"You and Joan? Really?"

"Stranger things have happened." He laughs and lifts us
off the ground.

I wonder if he knows about us, about our *stranger thing*
that happened.

I see you standing in the clearing waving before we
land. I wish I had a parachute. I can't get on the ground
quick enough.

When Beck touches down, my fingers are already pulling at the restraints. Beck reaches over to help, lifting the
headphones off of me. "Go to him!" he yells when he frees
the last buckle. "Go!"

I jump out and run while crouched over until I'm out
from under the blades. You're running toward me and
scoop me up over your shoulder when you reach me. We

spin around in circles, laughing. Then you slide my body down yours and take my face in your hands before kissing me, sweetly, deeply, thoroughly.

"My God, I've missed you Rachael." You wrap me in your arms and press my head against your chest.

"I've missed you too." I can't keep still and squirm away enough to take your hands. "I can't wait any longer to see the hotel!"

You smile with those dimples I'm addicted to. "Are you sure it's me you missed?"

I run my hand up the front of your shirt. "I'll show you how much as soon as you get me somewhere private."

"I know just the place."

You take my hand and lead me into the trees. I know where we're headed. Our secret spot. "The tree house?"

"The tree house." Your thumb strokes the top of my hand as we hike over brambles and fallen branches.

A brick patio comes into view lined with dozens of tiki torches. A wooden staircase with rope railings climbs up from the far end. "Merrick?" I rush forward. At the top of the stairs, a wraparound deck is filled with colorful flowers vining down over the sides in cascades of green leaves. The tree house has been completely rebuilt. A miniature A-frame house sits nestled in the limbs, the entire front is encased in glass windows. "It's like a fairy-tale house."

Your arms wrap around my waist from behind. "You like it then?"

I spin and gaze up into your dark eyes. "I love it. I can't believe you did this. Thank you."

"I'll never be able to give you enough." You kiss me softly and lead me to the stairs.

Up on the deck, the view of the island is the same as I remember from our picnic-that-wasn't. Our star gazing night. "I can taste chocolate cake when I stand here," I say, taking your finger and sliding the tip of it into my mouth.

You chuckle, and your eyes spark with desire. "I thought you might." You slide a glass door open and pull me inside the house. The bottom floor is one large room with a hot tub in the center, a plush white sofa on one side and a mini-bar on the other.

Beside the hot tub, there's a bottle of champagne chilling, two stemmed glasses and a chocolate cake with plump, red raspberries on top. "You never stop amazing me. Not for one second." A spiral staircase runs up the right side to the second floor. "What's up there?"

"The bedroom."

I slip my fingers under the waistband of your jeans and unsnap them. "Perfect."

With one quick tug, you have my sundress over my head and tossed to the floor. "Perfect," you repeat, running your eyes over my body.

I kick off my shoes at the same time you unhook my bra and strip me of my lace panties. You reach for me, but I skitter away, over to the hot tub and step into the bubbles. "Repeat performance, Mr. Rocha?"

You tear your t-shirt over your head and push your jeans and boxer briefs off while you stride over to me. "I'm thinking something new is in order, Miss. DeSalvo."

You step in beside me, but I don't let you sit. I scoop a handful of chocolate frosting off of the cake and cover your hard cock from tip to root. "Chocolate's never looked so appetizing." I take you in my mouth and your groan is fire to my soul. I've missed hearing you lost in your desire for me.

Your hands come to my head. I look into your eyes and whisper, "Take it. Take me, Merrick." You control our rhythm; my mouth and tongue absorb every thrust. When you speed and your hands grip and tangle in my hair, and you're so close the air rasps from your throat, you pull out.

"I don't want to waste it. I want to come inside you." I've been on the pill for a couple weeks now.

You kneel and kiss and suck the chocolate from my lips, lick it off my tongue. Your fingers find my center and slip inside, rubbing and stroking. "You're so wet already and not from the water."

"Getting you off turns me on."

You spin me around and pull me on your lap so we're back to chest. I shift so the head of your cock is at my entrance. You lift your hips and push inside me. It's heaven. I buck my hips to take you deeper, to feel you sliding in and out of me.

You hook your arms under my knees and glide us across the tub to the opposite wall. You guide me to where a jet shoots a hard stream of bubbles and rock me up and down so it massages my clit while you pump in and out of me.

"Oh my God," I whimper, letting my head fall back on your shoulder. I want it to last forever, but the rush starts building and burning inside me, and I come fast and hard reaching up and gripping your hair.

"Jesus, Rachael," you rasp. Your thrusts are harder and quicker and your body starts to shudder. You groan, and your cock throbs as my muscles clench around it. We're holding on to each other so tight, we might never come apart.

Your forehead rests against the back of my neck and you pull me across the hot tub. We recover in each other's arms, catching our breath and sharing feather-light kisses. "I have something to tell you," I say.

You run your hand up and down my back. "What is it?"

"You asked me to tell you when this happens." I smile. "Stockholm Syndrome. I'm falling in love with my captor, Merrick."

You press me against you hard and kiss me like your life is dependent on taking every breath with me. "You were my captor long before I was yours," you say, nuzzling against my cheek. "You captured my heart before I ever approached you."

You stand and step out of the tub, holding out your hand to me. "Come up to bed with me."

I take your hand and together, dripping wet, we pad up

the spiral staircase to the bedroom. It's all white walls, carpet and bedding with a king sized, mahogany poster bed in the very center. Sheer white drapes hang from the high bedposts. You lie in the center of the bed and open your arms for me. "One more surprise."

I climb on the bed and lie in your arms.

"Look up, you say, pointing to the ceiling.

I gaze up at the beam the runs the length of the ceiling where the slopes of the roof meet in the center. "Oh…" I cover my mouth with my hand and tears spring to my eyes.

Beside the etched letters A.W. plus I.B. with a heart around them is a fresh engraving, the letters M.R. plus R. D. surrounded by another heart.

I turn my gaze to you, meeting your deep, dark, blazing eyes. "You were right to bring me here. I am home."

Rachael and Merrick's story continues in:

No Takebacks

A Novella by Kelli Maine

Available now.

Continue reading for a sneak peek...

One

The sun beats down on us. It's hot. Sauna hot. The kind that makes the air heavy and saturates your skin with a sheen of moisture.

I let my eyes roam over your tan, sculpted chest down to where your fingers thread together resting on your abs.

"Like what you see?" you ask. Smiling, you reach out and trace your finger along my cheek. I wish I could see your eyes behind your black sunglasses.

"You know I do."

You chuckle and link your hands again, relaxing on your lounge chair.

The pool water ripples in the breeze, sunlight glinting off its surface. Pinkish-purple bougainvillea twines up to the palm frond roof of the pool-side bar. How did we get here? Us together. I never thought it would come to this. There were so many obstacles between us.

Over the past few months, Turtle Tear has been transformed from ancient ruins to luxury resort on a private island in the Everglades. In the distance, the work crew bangs and saws, finishing the last few rooms in the hotel.

"Let's cancel tomorrow," you say. "I don't want to share you."

"We've waited too long for this." Even though it's only

been about six months for me, you've waited years for this day to come. Tomorrow is the grand opening of Turtle Tear Resort to our friends and family. After that...well, I haven't decided if I want to open it to the public, or keep it private. I guess I'm not ready to share this place or you with anyone else either. "After they're all gone, you can become a hermit."

You take my hand and kiss it. "At least you promised me we could stay in the tree house and not crowd in the hotel with everyone else."

I roll to my side and run a finger down your arm. "I love our little hideaway."

Footsteps sound from the covered walkway. I sit up and turn to see Riley, your new assistant, step out from the shade and into the pool courtyard. "Why are you wearing dress pants and a tie?" I ask him. "Are you insane? It's sweltering out here."

You sit up, and your knees bump against mine. "Riley likes to look professional." You grasp the left side of my red bikini top and tug it closed. "And you're a little too casual. More like falling out."

"No interest in sharing me with this assistant then?" I whisper.

You clench your jaw, but don't reply. I was teasing, but struck a nerve bringing up the reason I left you last time.

"Ms. DeSalvo," Riley interjects, spots of pink on his cheeks from either the heat or from overhearing my comment, "your mother and aunt are scheduled to arrive at ten a.m.. tomorrow morning. Do you have a preference of which rooms are reserved for them?"

I shade my eyes and glance up at him, wishing I hadn't forgotten my sunglasses back in the hotel. "No. I'm sure you'll pick very nice rooms for them. I trust your judgment. But can you do me a favor?"

He nods, eager to please. "Of course."

"Call me Rachael."

A sheepish grin spreads across his face. He's young, twenty-two at most, not that I'm much older. But is reserved manner and uncontrollable blushing make him seem a lot younger. "Can I get you another drink from the bar, Rachael?"

I pick up my empty mimosa glass from the small table beside my chair and hold it out to him. "That would be amazing of you. Thanks."

"Mr. Rocha?" he asks, taking my glass.

You pick up your half-full bottle of water and shake it in Riley's direction. "I'm good, thanks. But that reminds me, when's the domestic staff getting in?"

"Three this afternoon."

Riley trots off toward the bar on the opposite side of the pool and courtyard. "Someone has a crush," you say, squeezing my knees between yours.

The stubble on your face has grown to a soft beard that covers your chin, not quite as full as it was when we first met, but soft to the touch and sexy. I can't resist running my fingers over it. "You're right," I say. "But look at him. Those pressed oxford shirts he wears, the flop of dusty blond hair over his forehead and the way he always blushes when he looks at me. How can I not be crushing hard?"

You lower your sunglasses to the end of your nose and arch one brow over your blazing, dark eyes. "You're full of jabs today, aren't you? You know what I meant."

I stand between your legs and take your face between my hands skimming my fingers through your dark, wavy hair. "You know I'm kidding. Look at you." I let my hands run down your neck, across your broad shoulders, down over the bulging muscles of each arm. "Why would I ever want anyone else?"

Your hands find my hips and pull me closer, close enough to rest your cheek against my stomach. "I've already done everything you're just getting to do. I've reached my goals. You could have someone like him—like you. Someone driven, making is way up the ladder. I kicked my ladder down, Rachael."

Why do you think I care that you've decided to retire in your mid-thirties with billions in the bank? Somehow in your head that's a bad thing. "You told me your plan months ago. When we went fishing, remember?"

"The storm that day." You chuckle, sending vibrations through my skin. "I swear, you wrapped your wet little body around my back so tight when I carried you back to the hotel, I had obscene images running wild in my head."

"Every time lightning flashed, I thought we were going to die." I stroke the top of your head, twisting sun-warmed locks of hair around my fingers. "The fish you caught was good though."

You turn your head and rest your chin in my bellybutton. "Yeah? You hardly touched it."

I bend and kiss the grin off your face. Eating around you leads to kissing you and touching you and meals are quickly shoved aside and forgotten. I've lost eight pounds since I stepped foot on this island. "We need another chocolate raspberry cake."

You growl and lick my stomach sending delicious flesh memories straight to my center. Memories of smeared chocolate frosting devoured with your tongue. "Don't worry. I've got that covered."

"Uh…" Riley stammers, standing at the end of my lounge chair with a fresh mimosa in one hand. "I'll just…" He sets it on the wooden table and shuffles away.

"Thanks!" I call after him. "Think he's a virgin?"

You let out a derisive snort. "Can't imagine why you'd think that."

"I don't know. Maybe he's just modest."

"Hmm. Maybe." With a flick of your fingers, my bikini top falls open. "Glad you're not."

"Not with you." I wrap my arms around your neck and you pull me down on top of you on the lounge chair sucking a nipple into your mouth.

"Ah," I gasp. I'll never get used to the feel of your lips, your tongue. It's too good, too drive-me-insane phenomenal.

I press against your shoulders, releasing my flesh with a drag of your teeth. I have to have your mouth on mine, your tongue sliding over mine drawing moans from deep in my throat.

I devour your lips. No holding back. I held back so long

waiting to trust you, but now I need to take and take and never stop until there's nothing left of you. Consume you delicious bite by delicious bite.

Rewarded with a low groan when I nip your bottom lip, I taste my way across your jaw to lap your earlobe and take it in my mouth. Your hands squeeze my ass and slide down between my inner thighs, pulling them apart so I'm strad-dling you. Your chest is warm under my splayed fingers, salty on the tip of my tongue tasting your hard pecs. You rock your hips into me. I dig my nails into your skin in response making you suck in an airy hiss through your teeth.

The wind blows my hair across your face, cools my bare back damp with heat. You ball my hair in your hands as I trail kisses down your stomach. "I love how you taste."

My hair goes loose around my shoulders and you run both palms down my back. "I never want anyone else here. Just us. Alone."

"Me too," I say, springing your hard length free from your swim trunks. "I'll have you naked whenever and wher-ever I want."

Your fingers find my nipples and begin pulling, pinch-ing and rolling, sending shocks of clenching arousal through my center. "My sex kitten."

I run my thumb up the thick vein running from the base of your cock to the ridge around the head. A bead of pre-come glistens at the tip. "Mmm, for me?" I tuck my hair behind my ear and lave your slit with my tongue while staring into your deep, dark eyes. "I love giving you that look on your face."

About the Author

While not sitting at her laptop writing romance novels or procrastinating on Pinterest, Twitter and Facebook, Kelli Maine can be found avoiding laundry, waging war with a dishwasher, strategically planning her vacation requests to get the most time off, and convincing herself she doesn't really want that dark chocolate Godiva bar.

Kelli loves hearing from readers! Find her on Twitter @KelliMaine, on her blog: www.kellimaine.blogspot.com, and on Facebook and Goodreads.